A BREACH IN TRUST 2

DCS Books and Publication, LLC

DAVID C STEWART

Table of Contents

CHAPTER 1

CAROL

My eyes wandered around my new office, but always seemed to rest on the gold nameplate on my scarred, mahogany desk.

My son, Kevin, had given me the nameplate a week ago, a day after I accepted the position at William Penn high school as its students' guidance counselor. It's still unbelievable to me what I've been able to achieve so far, but it had taken hard work at a diligent pace to get to this point. I had struggled through numerous awkward situations which many of the less fortunate students, here at the school, had gone through themselves and some who are still experiencing difficulties; plus, I'm where I have had some schooling myself. Now I'm back and anxious to try and assist those students I feel might need guidance.

My eyes again rested on the nameplate then on the bare egg-white walls and two metal file cabinets tucked in one corner.

I struggled to yank open the middle drawer of my desk. A note had been left inside. *"You asked for it."* the note read. It was signed by Mrs. Burns, an English instructor, who's been teaching at the school even before I was a student here. I checked the rest of the drawers for more surprises. They were empty. I settled into my chair and closed my eyes, thanked the Lord for his blessing to lift me from welfare and guide me to my feet. "God is good," I said aloud, ending my prayer.

At the small window, I surveyed a busy Broad Street. My childhood appeared behind my eyes so I pushed away my thoughts and dragged a box of personal items across the floor, items I hope will spruce up the empty office. My Certificate of bachelor's degree in Sociology and my Masters in Guidance Counseling from the University of Pennsylvania were the first items I grabbed. I smiled at the framed degrees before searching for the right places to hang them. "Not bad for a single mom from the projects," I said aloud. I decided to hang them directly on the wall behind the desk and above where my shoulders will be when I'll be counseling teens. I pulled another item from the box. It was a photo of myself and my three children. The twelve-year old twins, Kia and Kelly, and Kevin who'll be eighteen in December. I sat the framed photo on the desk just as a knock came at the door. Before I answered, Mrs. Burns stuck her salt and pepper head inside.

"Oh, good. You're here. Just checking. I wanted to know if you'd join me for lunch in the cafeteria?"

"Sure."

"Good. I'll hold us a table." She stepped inside. "Do you need anything more?"

"No. Thank you. I think the tour you gave me last week informed me plenty."

"Wonderful then." Her wide, brown eyes sparkled with delight. She spun in her black, floral dress and waved on her way out. "Don't hesitate to ask for anything," she threw over her shoulder.

The school's second floor hallway was cluttered with chattering teens giggling while mulling between classes. Their screaming shook my nerves, but I just kept moving and shaking my head and pushed through the crowds, listening, trying to decipher the beat-box noises, rapping, and young girls degrading other young girls by referring to them as bitches. Some girls covered their mouths when they noticed me eyeballing them. Then there were others, teenagers who kept on cussing as if they were grown alcoholics. Ninety percent of William Penn's students are minority; and it shows amidst the sea of black faces and the fashion show being exhibited. Baggy jeans and Timberlands for the boys and low-rider jeans and belly shirts for the girls. My eye for street fashion hadn't just developed. I'd been raised in ghettos most of my life, so, what I was observing was anything but unusual to me. I understood how brandishing high fashion can lessen the dislikes of black youths, can cause an urban youth to feel less unimportant amongst their peers and better about being without material things they assume their lives should possess.

I was passing the girls' bathroom when I noticed three girls eyeing me suspiciously. I decided to begin my reputation, "Is there a problem?" I asked.

"If it was, you'd know," one sassed.

I grinned, stepped toward the bathroom door. All three straightened their slouching.

"Somebody's using the bathroom," another said.

I split their line of defense. "I'm sure there's room for one more."

I entered the bathroom and was stifled by thick cigarette and marijuana smoke. The smoke was so thick, I fanned a hand across my face, blinked several times to ease the burning in my eyes.

Shock was on the faces of the ten or so girls who began stubbing their smokes and pretending to be doing makeup. Within seconds, the bathroom was nearly clear of students except for two girls. One girl I recognized from the Hank Gathers Community Center where I volunteer some weekends. She still fingered a cigarette. Her friend fingered a joint. They were quiet, staring at me as if I'd intruded on their turf, I hadn't expected this. - Now, I had little idea what to say. I said what my teachers had said to me when I used to hang in the bathrooms. "Don't you two have classes or something?" I managed. My heart sank when I noticed one girl's belly. I turned away to erase the flashbacks of my own past.

"It's fourth period lunch. Duh…" remarked the thin girl with slanted eyes and caramel skin. She stubbed out her joint and tucked it in her palm.

I held out my hand.

She gritted me up and down then rolled her eyes. "I'll talk to you later, girl," she said to her pregnant friend then started by me.

I stepped in front of her with my palm still out. Eye to eye we stood, sizing each other up. I had her by a couple of inches and outweighed her by twenty or so pounds. My heart was thumping, mostly from anticipation.

"Give it to her," said the pregnant girl.

Our eyes were still locked. When I reached for the joint, she let it drop to the floor.

"Oops," she slurred then passed by me with you ain't-said-nothing eyes.

I turned to the pregnant girl. "And you."

"And me what?"

"You plan on putting that cigarette out?"

She dragged the cigarette once more before letting it fall to the checkered linoleum floor, stumped it out with the toe of her black Reebok. "I know you, don't I?" she asked. "You work for the rec center, right?"

"No. I work here."

She wobbled to the sink and splashed water on her redbone skin.

"How old are you?" I asked.

She dried her face with some tissue. "Please, don't start preaching' 'bout no cigarette."

"I asked because I would like to know."

"Fourteen," she shrugged.

I folded my arms across my chest. "And your name is what?"

She tsked before rolling her eyes. "Felicia Knight."

I nodded as if I already knew her. "Well, Miss Knight, don't you think it's time you eased up with the nicotine and give the child you're carrying a chance?"

She didn't answer, just raised a palm, and walked by me. "Excuse me, Miss Knight," I called after her.

She stopped and spun. "Look, lady, I heard it all before, okay? I'd appreciate it if you just do what it is you do around here…monitor halls, bathrooms, or whatever. Don't even try preaching to me because you don't even know how many times, I heard those tired-behind lines." She spun back around and snatched open the bathroom door. "I got classes."

She left me there, staring at the door and wondering if I should've taken this job, wondering if I were cut out to shape the minds of young adults and prepare them for life beyond high school. I took a deep breath and exhaled. Time will tell.

Lunch with Mrs. Burns was awkward. She still lunches in the student cafeteria just as she had done when I was a student here. To be seated with her and sharing lunch as peers was intimidating. Sitting with her had me self-conscience about how I'd like to be perceived by the students as the newest staff member, a staff member that will have to gain students' trust to be effective at my job.

Mrs. Burns had been pointing out those she deemed to be "the bad kids." It wasn't her choices that bothered me so much as it was her conviction of having already counted them out.

The crow's feet at the corners of her eyes shown deeper as she was squinting with each word. She wore too much makeup, as she always has, and to me, with hearing her speak and watching her demeanor, I can see why some of the children feel intimidated by her.

"Look at that one." Mrs. Burns pointed with a cold stare. She was singling out Felicia, who'd entered the cafeteria with a group of four girls. They sat at one of the longer tables across the aisle from us. The conversation she and I had earlier in the bathroom came to mind. I bit into the cold burger I'd been nursing.

"They're all the same," said Mrs. Burns. "Babies having babies. Boys. Boys or babies. It doesn't matter. Kids today need to be ashamed of themselves."

"Do you know her?" I asked.

"I've seen her around. She and that dropout, Hasim Riley, be hugged up so much, you'd think they were Siamese twins."

"Is that whose baby she's carrying?"

"Who's to know. As fast as you think who's with who things change."

"Is that how you felt about me when I used to walk around this school pregnant?"

She fingered her neatly folded handkerchief and patted two red lips. "Probably. But you turned out well, now didn't you? I guess there are some exceptions, as there always are. But not many I suppose." She stood and smoothed her flowered dress. "There's ten minutes before the bell sounds. I like to beat the crowd. Are you situated?"

I nodded and remained seated.

"You were such a good student." She smiled warmly. "I'm pleased you've come back to help but take some advice. Don't become too involved in the children's' lives. It'll only bring you grief."

With that said, Mrs. Burns made her exit. For the life of me, I couldn't figure out if she were for the students or against them. I gave her the benefit of doubt. However, she had displayed a lack of confidence in whether there is hope for this new generation.

I spent the rest of my afternoon settling in my office until the 2:45 bell rang, signaling the end of the school's day. Staff would linger and mingle until 3:30, but I had been summoned to the principal's office.

Mr. Epps, the school's principal, is a small man with soft eyes and a warm smile. At five-foot-three inches, we would stand eye to eye, but he chose to speak with me from behind his desk in a too large leather chair.

I sat across from him.

"So, how did it go…your first day I mean?

"Well. Slow, but much like I thought it would. I haven't had time to review many of the children's files, but I will."

"Splendid. Glad you weren't spooked."

"Spooked?"

He grinned and leaned forward. Well, maybe spooked was the wrong word to use. What I mean is that your job at this school is one of necessity, Miss Shavers. As a first-year counselor with an enormous case load and equal responsibilities, it can be a bit intimidating."

I fought down my wanting to agree and sat quietly.

"I can remember my own initial impression of the school. But why bring that up. What's important is the perception you bring, this school's integrity, and its students. That's why I've chosen you for this job, out of love for these students." He stood and came around to the front of the desk. He rubbed his stubbled beard. His eyes were shinning. "You have what no other candidate for the position possessed. A purpose."

"Excuse me?"

"You know…purpose. A reason for wanting to see these children succeed. You've been in their shoes as well as in the trenches. You know their problems more-so than any book education can teach at any university."

I considered his words. His confidence in me nearly exceeded my own.

He returned to his leather chair. "Am I'm wrong?" he asked.

A tingling trickled through me. I knew that I had something to offer the students and knowing that Mr. Epps believes it as well is inspiring. Nothing teaches like real-life experience. What my college degree has taught me is how to implant the seeds in their minds. What seeds to plant and in which soil to plant them will be my hardest task. Some seeds may only produce weeds, and my experiences will have to guide me in order to produce flowers. No one understands a child of the ghetto better than a parent of a ghetto child.

Mr. Epps and I spoke for thirty minutes. I left the school assured that my "purpose" for seeking out my new career was achievable.

I had parked my leased Altima across from my office window.

As I eased the car into traffic, I gazed up at the window and blushed. I felt accomplished, so different from my old self. No longer will I have to depend on public assistance, public housing, or any man to motivate or mold me into a satisfied woman. Gratified is how I felt to be independent, and it had only taken five and a half years of educating myself to achieve this sensation. Of course, those years had not been at all easy—not with three children and a drug addicted babies' daddy all vying for attention.

I turned off Broad Street and slipped a CD in the dash. Maxwell's "Let's Stay Home Tonight" engulfed me. Immediately, I felt relaxed and I allowed the music to swallow me whole while the smoothness of the ride to mellowed me from the tensions of the first day on the job.

The neighborhood I'd moved into wasn't a huge step from the projects, where I used to live, but it's a step up, nonetheless. We've lived in the Germantown section of Philadelphia for two years, and already the advantages have outweighed the disadvantages by far. My number one consideration for moving here had been the crime rate. It's been a far less headache than when I was in the projects, simply because the poverty rate is less. Many of the homes on my street are owned by so-called middle-class families. As I am, most residents rent to own, and I figure if I'm thirty-one now, by the time I'm forty, I'll own my home outright. I've already begun renovating the two-story home by appealing to the city for vouchers to have the home wheelchair accessible for Kevin.

I stepped onto my front porch and cringed from the music thumping inside. On many occasions I've asked Kevin to respect our adjoining neighbors. I was near deafened by DMX's lyrics when I opened the door. I squinted, dropped my briefcase in the living room and bypassed the twins, sitting Indian style, on the living room floor playing jacks. I clicked the off button on the stereo and surveyed the living room. It was a mess. Bookbags and jackets covered the sofa and chairs. A mountain of penny candies lie scattered on the coffee table. Neither twin seemed enthused to have me home. They continued their game. "Where's Kevin?" I asked.

"Upstairs," they sang in unison.

"Ya'll get up from there and hang those jackets up. Take those bookbags to your rooms and tell Kevin I said to come down here."

Both girls stood, arguing over their game. I wondered if they'd say hello.

"Mommy, Miss Diane said she gonna be late picking' us up tomorrow from school. She gotta be at the doctor," said Kelly.

"How late?"

"I don't know," she shrugged as she gathered her jacket and bookbag then headed upstairs.

"Have you lost your tongue, Kia?" I asked.

"No."

"Then can you at least say hello?"

"Hi, Mom."

"'Hi, Mom,'" I mimicked as I passed through the dining room in route to the kitchen -- the largest room in the house. I had been surprised by the kitchen's enormity. It's one main reason why I had decided to purchase the home. I poured myself a glass of apple Snapple and started dinner. I was pulling the wrapping from a family-size pack of lamb chops, I'd set out to defrost this morning, when Kevin entered the kitchen.

Kevin sat tall in his wheelchair. He was his father's image with short, wavy hair and a thin build. His shoulders had widened since had begun lifting weights, but his smile still possessed its child-like innocence.

"How was it?" he asked.

"Strange. It would have been better if I knew that I could trust you not to blast the music while I'm gone."

Kevin rolled to where I stood and smiled. "Sorry."

"Mm-hm. I bet."

"I am. I went upstairs right before you got in. Plus…"

I cut his words short. Kevin, please…"

"Okay, okay. I'll put headphones on."

"Thank you." I turned back to the stove.

"I can make KK sandwiches if you want," Kevin offered.

KK is Kevin's nickname for the twins.

"No. It's okay. They had sandwiches three times this week already. Plus, you should be trying to get every meal possible. When you're on campus, you'll be missing these." I turned and blew him a kiss.

Kevin is so much like his father, Langston, who'd been killed in a car crash early during my pregnancy with Kevin. I had been thirteen then. Langston's death had crushed me.

"I'ma miss your cooking, Mom, but I'm still looking forward to being on my own for a while."

"You sure you know what you're asking for? Temple's a tough school. It's even tougher living on campus."

"I'll be fine."

The twins rushed into the kitchen; both were out of breath. "Mom, Kia pushed…pushed me…pushed me over the bed and cursed."

"Uh-uh, Mom. She storying! She mad 'cause…'cause she lost in jacks."

"Uh-uh. No, I didn't."

"Yes, you did."

I rested a hand on the counter and one on my hip. Lately, the girls would argue over anything. Games. TV. Clothes. Oh, Lord, can they argue over clothes. I used to buy them identical outfits until last year. That's when the fighting really escalated from shoves to wrestling then punches. Kia's always been more aggressive and is usually the one who I chastise most. "Did you two do your homework yet?"

"No," Kia answered. Kelly shook her head.

How could they be alike and yet so different? I thought. "Then I want the two of you to take your narrow behinds upstairs, and get it done. Do I make myself clear?" They nodded.

"I don't want to see your faces or hear you until I call you for dinner. I'm tired of the fighting."

They pouted then moped from the kitchen. I returned to dinner.

"It's been that kind a day, huh?" asked Kevin.

"No. But it doesn't make sense the way they argue."

"They're probably tired of looking at each other. Every time they look in the mirror, they see each other's face."

"Thank goodness. I don't know if I could take two Kevins."

We both smiled.

After dinner, I went over the girls' homework with them. Math mostly I felt good about how both have grasped the concept of mathematics, and the fact that they compete against one another to learn the most. It suits me simply fine. One is always showing off, anxious to tell the other how to do a problem. Both are a trip.

Kevin retired to the computer in his room, and after I showered, I retired to my room as well. I had brought home a few of the students' files, those who I planned on speaking with tomorrow, students' whose files bear red dots next to their names. The previous counselor had taken "special" interest in these students, and from what I could tell, just from reading the few files I've read already, she had no choice. I found myself wondering about Felicia. Tomorrow I'll look over her file, too. Maybe I'll give her my own red dot. There has to be a story there.

CHAPTER 2

WESLEY

My idea of a good time is opposite Pam's family's ideas. This is the third party — excuse me — "bash" they've thrown in two months. All three have carried the same theme. Boring. The only difference, that I could recognize, is the food selections. The forty or so guest always seem quite republican. Suited and booted. Evening gowns. Lots and lots of money.

Business deals and promises were quietly being made around the room. This I was sure of.

Pam's parents are high society African Americans, who've had money way, way too long, so long, in fact that, their ideologies are no longer Black. I've always wondered if they ever were. Now that I stand across the room from Pam, who's chatting it up with a guest, I can see so much of her parents in her. I surveyed the over-forty crowd and finished off my Bacardi and coke. I made my way to the bar and ordered another. "Well, hello," a voice purred behind me.

I turned to face Mrs. Ingram, an attorney with Winthrop Industries, who was staring down at me. She was mid-fiftyish and extremely tall. An easy six foot five. "Mrs. Ingram, how are you?"

"Just fine." She set her empty goblet on the bar top.

"Cognac," she said to the bartender then slide beside me, flashing much cleavage. She'd made a pass at me once before. I knew she had an agenda.

"How's Mr. Ingram?" I asked, diverting my eyes.

"Boring as usual. All he thinks about is work and boating. Drives me mad."

I knew her husband well. He draws up many of Winthrop Industries' life insurance plans, and my being Marketing Director for the corporation, we've sat and strategized during Board meetings.

"I thought the two of live on a boat?"

"We do. So, why talk about what we already have? I'd like to talk about thing's that I'd like to have." Her tone was seductive.

The bartender returned with our drinks, which gave me back the personal space she'd been easing into.

I raised a toast to her. "To new adventures," I said. She gave a sly smile. "I wish."

I watched Mrs. Ingram slither away just as Pam arrived beside me.

Pam looked extremely vibrant in her blue satin and lace gown. Her makeup was perfect. "Are you bored yet?" she asked.

"Bored's not the word."

"Even with old-lady Ingram sweating you?" Pam teased.

I smiled. "And what makes you think that?"

"It's documented that she prefers her boy-toys young and successful." Pam began straightening the bowtie of my tux.

"Don't worry. I'm not interested."

"You better not be." She pecked my lips. "Let's get out of here. If I hear one more Dionne Warrick song, I'm going to pull my hair out at the roots."

"I'm with that."

"Let me just say bye to Daddy."

Pam's parents were across the room. Pam led me through the crowd by the hand, much like when I had first visited their home six years ago. I have to admit that Mrs. Winthrop has aged well at forty-nine. She resembles Natalie Cole, only lighter, with hazel eyes and short hair.

Mr. Winthrop can easily pass for Steve Harvey's dad. Real country, with silver sideburns. The Winthrops spends a fortune on jewelry. Each time I speak with them, my eyes remain glued to their huge diamond wedding bands and Mrs. Winthrop's twelve-carat diamond engagement ring. They were speaking with Judge Creighton when Pam interrupted.

"Daddy. Mom. Wesley and I are leaving."

Their attentions turned toward us. "Leaving?" asked Mrs. Winthrop. Her smile never faltered, but if you knew her, you'd know she was hiding her embarrassment. She turned to the Judge. "Judge, you remember our daughter, Pamela?"

"Certainly. Hello again, Pamela."

"...And her fiancé, Wesley Rhodes," said Mrs. Winthrop. "Mr. Rhodes," greeted the judge.

"Wesley's also Winthrop Industries' Eastern Regional Marketing Director," added Mr. Winthrop.

"Really?" The judge's eyebrows rose a bit.

"So, when's the date?" asked the judge. "I'll be happy to perform the ceremony."

"We aren't certain as of yet," answered Pam. "Soon though."

"Great. This country needs more young couples. I wish the both of you success."

"Thank you," replied Pam.

We stood with stilled smiles until Mr. Winthrop cleared his throat. "Well, now...Wes, my boy...are you set for your trip home?"

I hadn't told him about my trip to Philly. I turned to Pam, who innocently looked away. "Yes, sir. I'm all set."

"And how long will you be gone?"

"A week, maybe. Of course, I'll only be a phone call from the office."

"Nonsense. Enjoy your brother's wedding. We're not asked to be best man often in our lives."

"Thank you, sir."

"No. It's you I need to be thanking for keeping my baby girl smiling."

"Daadddy!" Pam whined.

"Oh hush, Pamela," added Mrs. Winthrop. "Your father loves you."

Pam tsked and grabbed my wrist, "if you're done embarrassing me, I think I'll go now." Pam turned to the judge. "It was wonderful to see you again, Judge Creighton."

"You as well, Pamela."

I said my goodbyes as well, and in minutes, Pam was pulling me down the elaborate driveway to her BMW. We stopped so that she could step out of her high heels.

"God, I hate these parties" Pam said.

"You could've fooled me. You seemed to be enjoying yourself."

"It's all about appearances, Wesley. Creating a good rapport for situations that might arise later."

"I still think you have a good time."

She frowned and tossed her car keys to me. "You drive."

That was fine with me, being she drives like a maniac, and I'd watched her down way too many Martinis.

Inside the car, Pam slipped an Usher CD in the stereo and began winding her hips to the music.

I shook my head and grinned. "Every time you drink, you get freaky."

"And…?"

"Nothing. I just made an observation."

"Don't even play, Wesley. You giving me some when we get home." She leaned over and turned up the music, probably to drown my reply.

It's been Pam's way throughout most of our relationship. She's extremely good at getting what she wants, when she wants it, especially from me. She has a knack at making you feel guilty and wanting to give her your all. Even during our lovemaking, which is usually intense, I find myself replenishing my fluids with protein drinks. I'd consider Pam a freak in the bedroom. But, outside of the bedroom, she's straightforward and business minded, sometimes cold and downright intimidating. Without a doubt, she's as spoiled as they come. I'd blame her father's fortune. He and I seem to be the only men who manage to crack her hardened exterior.

After a long passionate kiss outside of our apartment's door, we entered our apartment with Pam's head resting against my shoulder. She was still barefooted and dropped her shoes to the thick carpet. "I am soooo glad to be home," she churned.

I tossed the door keys on the foyer table and loosened my tie.

Pam had made her way to the living room bar and was pouring herself a drink.

"Haven't you had enough?" I asked.

She stretched out on the velour sofa. "Oh, God. Please, don't start with me."

I sat beside her and lifted the glass from her fingers. "You've had enough already."

She pouted. It was times like these when Pam craves to be babied. I've seen her fail trying to out drink the best of them, so, her little I'm-so-vulnerable act, I knew, was a play for attention. She draped her arms around me. "Don't leave me, baby," she crooned.

"I'm not going anywhere, Pam."

"Yes, you are."

I pecked her martini-tainted lips. "No. I'm not."

"You're going to Philly for a whole week."

"What's one week?"

"A week when I'll be alone. A week you won't be at my Fashion Review."

"So, that's what's wrong, huh? Is that what all your purring and whining is about? You want me at your show?"

Her coal eyes saddened, and her lips tightened. She pushed me away. "So, what I want you there? You are my man, aren't you?"

I readied myself for an argument. "We've been through this.

The wedding is next week and I gotta be there for Stacks."

"I just bet you do, Mr. Best Man. And I bet you're going to be there for the Bachelor Party, too?" Pam rose and stomped off toward the bedroom.

I looked on, told myself that she's tripping. Her jealousy has gotten totally out of hand lately. Right now, my concern is being there for my brother on his wedding day, and that's what I intend to do.

The air conditioning in Winthrop Inc. has been broken since 9 a.m., and my office was moist because of the outside humidity.

I had just closed the last file that had needed my immediate attention, and had given Vanessa, my secretary, her instructions when Julius strolled in. I tossed my company pen on the desk and clasped my hands behind my head, waiting for the huge smile to fall from his face.

"Off to Philly, huh?" he asked.

"Yep."

Julius McCray is Winthrop's key computer technician and is always dapper in expensive suits. Today he was sporting a tailored Brook Brothers. He's what Pam calls all-tall-and-light-skinned. "Wes, my man, you better be careful."

"About what?"

"That love bug."

"Love bug?"

"You better know it. First, you're the best man, then the groom."

I grinned. "I'm not that superstitious."

He helped himself to a seat in the straight back across from the desk, still smiling.

Since I began working for the company, we've been tight. It wasn't until later that I found out that he'd been sizing me up because he had a major crush on Pam before she took off for college at Temple.

"I'm just forewarning you. When you get back in town, and find yourself proposing to Pam, don't say I didn't warn you."

"J, you be bugging." I shuffled some folders and began locking up my desk. When I looked up, Pam was standing in the doorway holding a single rose.

Julius turned to see what had grabbed my attention. He turned back to me and pointed. "See. Told you."

"Am I interrupting?" Pam asked, draped in a black sundress, black headscarf, and dark shades.

"Uhm…no. Julius was just leaving." I came from behind the desk and shook Julius's hand while escorting him to the door. He mouthed the words, "I told you so," just as I was closing the door on him.

"What brings you down here?" I asked Pam.

She removed the shades. It was obvious she'd been crying.

I wondered if this would be her last stand at getting me to stay.

"I was upset over how I acted last night." She extended the flower to me. "This is for you."

I accepted the rose and eyed it, confused. "I'm not upset with you, Pam."

"That's not the point. The point is that I've been selfish and hadn't considered your feelings."

I waited on the lightning bolt to strike her dead. I smiled. "You've been drinking, right?"

She cut a serious eye at me. "Just kidding."

"Well, don't. I'm trying to apologize."

"But you don't have to."

"You sure we're all right?"

"Positive."

"Then you aren't going to leave me?"

I shook my head. "Never crossed my mind."

"You treat me too good," she purred. "In that case, I'll be waiting for you to hurry home."

When the plane touched down at Philadelphia International, I felt as if Atlanta were years ago. Six years it's been since I've set foot in my hometown, and the good and bad about being back rose to the forefront. The good being, finally seeing my brother and Magic again. The bad is having to rehash memories of Benny's death. Also, I'll have to again face the past that I've been running from for so long. Although I have faced some of the horrors that still at times haunt me. It's hard to forget or even forgive myself for having been caught out there.

I made it through the airport's baggage claims and grabbed the first available cab willing to trek through the ghetto to Stack's crib. The driver was a brother with an artist's mustache and goatee.

"Have you been to Philly before?" he asked as we pulled from the curb.

"I grew up here, so, don't think about taking the long routes."

He laughed. "Do I seem like that kind a brotha?"

"I learned the hard way not to judge people by their looks."

"I hear you."

We rode south Broad Street to City Hall then circled the city's symbol until we were on Broad Street northbound. I took to the scenery with more emotion than I had anticipated. I had missed being around so many of Philly's familiar sights. My last experiences in the city weren't exactly heart-warming ones, and as we passed the State Building and Benjamin Franklin high school, I felt a nervousness overcome me. I've never gotten over the murder of my brother, Benny, and I don't think I ever will.

"So, how long you been away from the city?" the driver asked, trying to make small talk.

"Six years."

"Long time. Why'd you leave?"

I shifted in the back seat and gave the answer I had trained myself to give. "It's a long story."

He nodded. "Well, you seem to have done well."

I thought about that. "'Well' is a good word. But, for me, success includes happiness."

"Ahhh. I feel you, my brother. True that, true that."

The afternoon was hot, a desert dry. I rolled up the car window to avoid the outside heat. "You don't have AC up in here?" I asked.

"Nope. Broke."

Now that's sad, I thought. Here it is, one of the hottest days of 2002, and I picked a cab without AC.

We had entered the inner-city neighborhoods. Much of the property now belongs to Temple University. My Alma Mater. Huge burgundy banners with embroidered white T's waved from flag poles and streetlights. Even after we'd turned off of Broad Street and onto West Diamond, more of Temple's banners waved from brownstones' windows and light poles.

"How far down should I go?" the cabby asked.

"Eighteenth is cool."

At 18th Street, I had the cab turn on to Van Pelt Street and halt in front of Stacks' two-story rowhome. I paid the

man grabbed my few bags and watched him speed on up the street. All I could do is shake my head.

Before I reached the curb, Stacks' front door flew open, and he leaped the five steps, shouting. "Yeah, niggah, what? My mutherfuckin' niggah is in the hizouse! Whassup, Whassup, Whassup?" He bear-hugged me with all the trimmings, grabbed one of my bags, and escorted me into the house.

I couldn't believe all the weight he had picked up over the years. He'd gone from one-hundred and forty-five pounds

soak and wet to close to two hundred. "I see Denise been feeding you well." I nodded towards his round belly.

He palmed his gut. "Yeah. Big girl been lookin' out for a niggah."

"More like cooking out."

Denise entered the living room, toting two potted ferns dangling from clothes hangers. Denise was tall and heavy, with a pretty face and bright brown eyes. When she walks, her hips swing hard, makes you think that if she bumps you, you'll stumble for sure. "Hey, Wes, how you doing, baby?" she asked.

"I'm fine. How you been?"

I hugged her. "Congratulations. You finally broke my little brother down, huh?"

"Honneey, it's me who finally broke. He knew the deal.

No marriage until he got outta that life."

I turned to Stacks and raised my brows. "Yeah?" Stacks shrugged. "I had to get out sometime, right?"

Relief seized me. For years, I've been trying to lure Stacks out of the drug game, ever since our brother, Benny, had been murdered in retaliation for the crimes we'd committed nearly ten years ago. We'd been in the coke game heavy back then, but since that tragic day, I've vowed to turn my life around and have been pushing Stacks to do the same.

"How long do you plan on staying?"

"A week."

"Where?"

"Maybe my old place or the Double Tree."

"Uh-uh. You'll stay right here with us," Denise replied. "We have a spare room, food, or whatever. Ask your brother how Magic done turned your place into some bachelor pad."

"Nah. Say he didn't."

"Yeah. He did," added Stacks. "You should see it."

"No, the hell you shouldn't," spat Denise as she bounced by and out of the room. Her eyes had scolded Stacks.

"Yeah, Machiavelli…I see she got you on lockdown." Stacks slumped in his seat.

"She frontin."

"Mm-hm." I thought back to Stacks' archaic views toward women and relationships, views that had seemed deeply embedded.

Benny's death and my leaving for Atlanta had obviously steered him more toward Denise and how genuine her love for him was.

However, I wasn't about to give props to Stacks so quickly. I feel certain that the same old Stacks was lurking. I decided to ask. "So, what made you wanna get married?'

He shrugged. "Big girl. She just been doin' her thing. Lovin' a niggah, givin' a brotha her all. She deserves to get the thing she want most. Plus, I'm feelin' her like that."

All I could do is nod and take him at his word. If he wasn't in love with Denise, he certainly wouldn't've asked her to marry him. I don't care how well she cooks.

"What about you, Wes? Whassup with you and Pam? I'm kinda surprised she let you rip and run for a week."

I smiled. "Believe me…it wasn't easy. But she slowed down some."

"I find that hard to believe. She done highjacked your ass in Atlanta for six years."

"Man, what I say?"

Stacks snatched a Hennessey from a six-pack ring. "You talk your ass off, but I ain't mad at ya, 'cause lately, Big girl be havin' me hostage in the crib my damn self."

We both laughed.

"Wesley, the phone!" Denise called from the other room. I looked at Stacks, who had a smirk on his face.

"Don't worry, this'll be you in a week from now," I said before picking up the living room phone.

It was Pam.

CHAPTER 3

CAROL

I stuffed two more thick folders with red dots in my accordion folder. I'll read them at home. For two hours, I've been skimming through the thin files, somewhat familiarizing myself with several students' histories as quickly as possible. Transition of the position I've taken would have me behind already.

Most of William Penn's students come from poverty-stricken homes, inner-city neighborhoods that have caused many of the files read alike: single parents, abuse, neglect. Always with one or more of these traits, a pattern, it seems, that has captured these teens' self-esteems and has twisted them until the students crack beneath the enormous pressure. Some students here feel unimportant, abandoned, and disinterested in college or a lifelong career.

I'd just completed reading a thin file when a tiny knock came at the office door. "Come in," I called.

The somber face of a pudgy student entered. Her eyes were sad. "Hi," she mumbled without lifting her eyes from the floor.

My gaze wandered there as well. On their way, I noticed her haphazard attire. Old blue jeans. Old Converses, and a faded-pink floral shirt. Her hair was in two raggedy braids front to back. She was my first student visitor. Every college professor I'd listened to, who'd prepared me for this moment, flashed behind my eyes.

"Come on in," I said.

She shuffled inside and stood before me.

"Are you all right?" I asked.

She nodded. I was unsure if she'd smiled.

"Have a seat." I pointed her to the straight back beside the desk and watched her take in the office.

"What's your name?"

"Kyra. Kyra Mitchell."

I tried recalling her file. I hadn't read it yet. "And who's your homeroom teacher?"

"Mr. Roth."

"You're in the tenth grade, then?"

"Mm-hm."

"Well, Kyra, I'm Miss Shavers. Can I help you with something?"

She scanned the room again.

I leaned closer, trying to soothe her. "Don't worry. I can keep a secret."

"I'm quitting school," she blurted.

I leaned back, rolled to the file cabinet to find Kyra's file. I rolled back to the desk to read.

Mrs. Spellman, the former counselor, had kept brief notes and gaped entries. According to last year's grades, Kyra was academically sound, a bit shy and withdrawn. Her home-life is unstable, and her immediate kin is listed as her grandmother.

I laid the file on the desk and wondered…While reading I noticed Kyra fidgeting with a thin silver bracelet around her wrist. "Kyra, your file says you're an excellent student. Why would you want to leave school?"

She shrugged. "I hate it here."

"What exactly do you hate?"

She toyed with her bracelet.

I waved to recapture her attention. "Kyra, look at me, please?"

She puffed an exasperate breath but did as I asked. "What's the problem? Other students?"

She shook her head. "Not all of 'em."

"Girls?"

She chewed on her bottom lip. "Do other girls talk about you?"

She nodded.

"What are they saying?"

Tears began to swell in her eyes "Everything. Every fat joke. They talk about my clothes, my hair. They hate me."

I inhaled and slowly exhaled. "Whew! I thought we had a major problem."

Kyra looked befuddled.

"Kyra, aren't you smart enough to recognize jealousy when you see it?"

She only stared.

"People talk about others when they're not satisfied with themselves. They pick on people they believe are weaker. Do you think you're weaker than they are?"

"No."

"Do you think you're just as smart?"

"I don't know."

"Well, from the grades I just saw, I'm sure there aren't a lot of tenth-graders smarter than you."

She smiled and sniffled. "Then why do they pick on me?"

"Because, Kyra, they're jealous. They see you and know that they may never be as smart as you, polite, or even as beautiful inside without them having to put on an act. They see you without all of the hang-ups and peer pressure that they deal with every day." I reached for Kyra's hand. "Sweetheart, you don't want to drop out of school and ruin your future because of a few dingbats, do you?"

"No. But it hurt when they tease me all the time."

"Honey, I wish I had the perfect answer for you, but I don't. You can either hold your head up high and be proud of yourself, or you can run and hide your head in the sand your entire school years."

Kyra and I spoke for another ten minutes. I had given her a few tips that might help her appearance to lessen the ridicule.

I had just opened a red dotted file when another knock came at the door.

"Come in.

A teenage boy with a huge overbite and ashy skin entered the office. His hair was short and beady with a ragged hairline. Obviously, he hadn't visited a barber in months.

"Hello." I greeted.

He handed me a stained envelope and stood waiting while I read.

It was a letter from Mr. Epps informing me that Marcus Toole is returning from suspension for fighting and needs counseling.

"Welcome back, Marcus." His lips twisted a hello.

"We haven't met. I'm Miss Shavers, the school's new counselor."

He surveyed the bare office.

"Needs decorating, huh?"

He nodded.

I came from around the desk to where he stood. He was a few inches shorter than me. I hadn't reviewed many of the children's files, but Marcus's I had.

Marcus personifies the stereo-typical youth growing up in an inner-city environment. His mother, a seasoned crack addict, had abandoned his needs soon after his birth, and his father's currently serving a life sentence. Marcus's grandmother has the will to raise him, but without the strength to discipline, financial assistance, or an ability to keep an eye on Marcus's five siblings as well, Marcus has to fend for himself.

"I hope your fighting days are behind you, Marcus? Too many suspensions and you'll be a prime candidate for Boone."

"So, long's nobody mess with me, I won't fight."

"I know. And that's good. But you also have to not take everything somebody says or does so seriously."

"They need to shut up then." I breathed deeply.

Marcus would be one of many that I'll see much of. I walked back behind the desk and picked up the letter. "Your homeroom's been changed. You're in Mrs. Dixon's room now. Three seventy-five, okay?"

He nodded.

"How's everything at home?" I asked.

He shrugged and headed for the door.

"Marcus."

He turned back to me.

"If there's anything you need to talk about, it's okay to stop in."

He nodded and left.

Two more students visited me before lunch. A boy-crazed senior and a six-feet, four-inch eleventh grader who had been friends with my son, Kevin, when we had lived in Raymond Rosen projects. After recommending plenty birth control to the eleventh grader and updating, Lenny, Kevin's friend, on how Kevin's been doing and his plans for college, I felt drained and not at all ready for lunch with Mrs. Burns.

Lunch with Mrs. Burns was as I had expected. She'd gone through her lunch-time ritual of identifying the bad students and the promising ones. She'd even gone as far as criticizing most of the school's staff. She had especially strong criticisms for the Philadelphia School Board. I'm fairly new to the public-school system, so I didn't question much of what she'd said.

She's been around far longer. It became clear to me that things are certainly different from the inside looking out.

I spent the rest of the afternoon, uninterrupted, at my desk reviewing files. Some files without red dots, I placed red dots on. A few of the students' stories were heartbreaking and unbelievable, made me question my own troubled past as I reread through the horrors of abuse and abandonment, drug addiction and poverty. What also concerned me was that many of the students were reading on a sixth-grade level.

Now, as I walk the halls at the end of the day, every student I pass, I wonder if he or she is of the lot being pushed through the public-school system. It was just my second day on the job, and I was already depressed. I now understood what Mrs. Burns meant by the note that read: *"You asked for it."*

When evening arrived, I found myself trying to forget about work as I joined the seven volunteers scattered throughout the basement of the Mission Baptist Church. We were folding clothes and preparing care packages for financially strapped families.

I had begun volunteering at the church during my senior year of college and between volunteering at the church and rec center on Tuesdays and Fridays, there's been no greater reward. Just working in the trenches with teens and helping them through their struggles has lifted my spirit. Over time, I've become close to many church members and have recently been considering joining the church.

I shoved two wool sweaters in the hefty-bag I was packing and smiled at the twins sloshing paint on a banner for the church's upcoming bake sale.

"Sister Shavers, thank you for coming in today and helping out." Pastor Riley had come from behind me. A gray-haired woman who could double for Nell Carter.

"You're welcomed."

She glanced around the basement. "So, where's Kevin today?"

"He and a friend had other plans."

"And work...? I hear you've accepted the counseling job at Penn."

"Oh, God, yes. And work's...well, work's too soon to form an opinion about."

"Well, I'm glad the children now have such a wonderful person to help guide their souls."

"Thank you, Pastor."

We stood silent a moment.

"Well...I'll let you get back to your task now. There's so much that needs to be done."

I smiled graciously and watched Pastor Riley move to the next volunteer.

It was after eight when the twins and I made it home. I was beat tired and ready for a long, hot bath when the phone rang.

Kia answered it, spoke for a few minutes then called Kelly to the phone.

It could only be James on the phone, I thought. Plus, Kia gave him away with her wide grin and side-long glances towards me. She always tries to entice me to accept James back into our home. I wasn't having it. James had made his choice and had chosen the life of a dope fiend.

I looked away from Kia and Kelly's smiles and remembered how buttery James's words seemed when I was young, too.

"Mommy, Daddy wanna talk to you," Kelly said, extending the phone to me.

I held out my hand, so she'd bring the phone to me. I wasn't about to go to him in any way. I'd chased behind James's ass for too many years.

"What?" I asked into the receiver and watched the twins run upstairs.

"How you doing?"

"Fine."

"Good. That's good. Listen…I haven't been able to make it up that way in a while, and I might be able to stop by this weekend…to you know…see the kids I mean."

"I don't think so, James. Hold on a minute." I pulled the phone from my ear. "Kia, hang up the damn phone!" I yelled upstairs. I listened to the upstairs line click off. "We have plans this weekend with the church," I told James.

"The church?"

"Yeah. The church. If you pay more attention to what's going on in your daughters' lives, you'd remember we volunteer there."

James was quiet a moment. "Oh. Yeah, I remember. Okay then…then when can I see them?"

My mind raced to find a few languages in which to say "NEVER!"

"I don't know, James. Have you been going to your meetings?"

"Yeah. I've been going."

"Mm-hm. Well, I don't know when'll a good time be, but I'll let you know." I hung up the phone without giving him the chance to respond. As far as I'm concerned, he blew his chance six years ago when he had tossed his children aside, robbed us, and mentally abused us. Janice, James's mother, had told me that he was trying to get himself together, although, I'm not as naive to believe that. But Janice is. In her eyes, he's still her baby. In my eyes, he's a dead-beat dad.

I checked the wall clock and decided to page Kevin since I had the telephone in hand. Although he'll be going off to college soon, he still has a curfew to adhere to. I replaced the phone receiver and waited for Kevin to call back.

Kia sat beside me and rested her head in my lap. "I'm tired, Mommy."

"I know, baby. Mommy's tired, too."

I began toying with the baby-hair running across her ear and closed my eyes, wondered if I'd ever be able to trust another man.

CHAPTER 4

FELICIA

For the first time today, I felt my baby kick. The pangs from the wallop were just beginning to subside. When my fingers began aching from braiding Hasim's hair.

We were outside, on the stoop of Hasim's sister's rowhome, the place where Hasim sells his dope—right out in the open. The crew: Peaches, Tara, and Tiara were posted up around us. Tara and Tiara are sisters, and both are coupled with two of Hasim's homeboys who were also among us. In all, there are eight of us on the stoop and four 40-ounce bottles of Old English were being passed around. Everyone was drinking but me. Hasim calls himself not letting me drink because I'm carrying his baby, but little do he know, I haven't the slightest desire to drink while pregnant -- but I still smoke weed and reached for the blunt being passed around.

"Dang, Felicia," said Tiara. "It just got passed to me."

"I know you better not mess my hair up," Hasim warned
me before going up on a 40-ounce.

"I ain't mess it up, yet. Have I?"

"'Cause you know better."

I playfully pushed his head to the side. "Yeah right."

I took a few drags from the blunt and passed it down to Hasim. "Thanks, bay."

Hasim had been my first and only sexual partner. We've known one another for as long as I can remember. His mother and mine used to be best-friends, stripped at the same clubs, and even dated one another's ex — until Hasim's mother was found dead on a back street near a strip-club where she'd been working. It turned out that she had been prostituting.

"Hold up, Lisha. A customer comin'," said Hasim.

I reached into the front of my pants, into my panties and handed Hasim his stash. Hasim feels it's best hidden there because most nares are men and aren't allowed to frisk women, let alone a teenage girl. It also helps that I'm pregnant.

After Hasim served his customer, he sat back between my legs and handed me the stash.

"Turn to the side some," I told him as tucked away the baggie.

"I wish you hurry up and get done," Hasim pleaded. "I got shit to do."

Hasim's homies, Mookie, and Cal, began beat-boxing and rhyming. Tara and Tiara started doing the Harlem Shake while everyone else nodded in rhythm. An easy mood set on by the weed and beer.

After two more braids, I was done with Hasim's hair.

I was thankful, too. The afternoon sun seemed to be melting my skin, and I was ready to go indoors. I stood and stretched my back, took in the square of rowhomes and tarred, glassed- infested ground. There were a few adults perched on their stoops enjoying the afternoon. But mostly there were children riding bikes, skipping double-Dutch, or playing hopscotch.

Across the way, Shelly, a big-butt-and-a-smile, was with two whorey girlfriends, eyeing us. She and Hasim were hooked up once, but the way the two carry on at times, you'd think they were still a couple. I caught Hasim staring in her direction. "Is somethin' over there you want?" I asked Hasim.

He snatched his eyes in my direction. "Huh?"

"Is something the fuck over there you want?" I repeated.

"Lisha, don't start trippin', okay?"

"Mm-hm." I pushed past him. "I'm going to the store." I turned to Peaches and Celeste. "Ya'll comin?"

With half-opened, red, and glazed eyes, my best friends raised from the stoop and began gathering their bearings.

"Aww, Lisha," Peaches groaned, "don't nobody feel like walking."

"I'm goin', girl. I need a Pepsi to flush this beer," said Celeste.

"You wrong, Lisha," Hasim said.

I handed him his stash and strolled off. My main reason for stepping off was my displeasure with his infidelity. My girls know me best, and during the walk to 10th Street, they were trying to console me by criticizing all men.

"How the hell do they expect us to feel?" Peaches was saying. "They be all up in those bitches faces, like don't nobody know that they tryin' to wax that ass."

"Niggahs ain't shit!" Celeste added.

I'm a true red bone. Celeste is caramel-skinned, and Peaches is a deep chocolate. Just as different as our skin tones are our views about men. Being the youngest of our trio, at fourteen, I always find myself being schooled by the two sixteen-year-olds.

"Ya'll just sayin' that 'cause ya'll dykes," I said.

"Honey, ain't nobody no dyke," insisted Peaches. "Going both ways don't make you no lesbo."

"Coulda fooled the hell outta me," I joked.

Celeste knew to keep her mouth shut. The entire project knows she's a certified lesbian. Thankfully, because they're my girls and know that I don't swing both ways, they respect my preference.

We returned from the store and found Hasim gone. His boys, Tiara, and Tara were still on the stoop getting blunted and drinking. It was unlike Hasim to leave the get-high party.

"Where's Hasim?" I asked.

The four of them shrugged and looked at me cock-eyed.

My eyes wandered to where Shelly had been flaunting herself. She was gone, probably had been waiting for me to fade so that she could lure Hasim away. I turned back to the group. "Ya'll ain't shit!" I spat, grabbed at my belly, and stomped off.

Peaches and Celeste were behind me.

I only knew that my girls were behind me because of their cussing. They were saying things like: "I tol' you he wasn't shit, girl!" "You don't need him!" "I hope his dick fall off!" Having already suspected that Hasim was unfaithful made my assumption less painful; although, it still hurt like hell, especially since I'm carrying his child and have always been faithful to him.

My mom had gone ballistic when she found out that I was pregnant by the twenty-two-year-old. She warned me that Hasim was just using me for sex, and when he tires of that, he'll move on. Her words, etched in my mind, weren't helping any, they were confusing me.

I can't remember whose idea it was to walk to Progress Plaza. It's just something that the three of us do when we start to walking. We figure that something will grasp our attention. Today, a small clothing store held our interest. We had boosted a few short sets from the store once before, and when Peaches opened the front door, we all knew the deal. We spread out among the displays of skirts, blouses, and dresses, began acting as if we were in awe of everything we pick up.

"Ooohh, girl! Check 'this' out. My man will kill me if I squeeze my big behind in this," Peaches said. She was fingering a tiny, sheer blouse. "Ooohh, Miss…do you got this in an eighteen?" she asked the lone attendant.

The enthusiastic white woman came from behind the counter with "cha-ching" stapled on her aging face.

"This here is mine!" Celeste yelled, loud enough to spin the woman's attention to her. She'd picked out a lavender pants-suit and was modeling it against her body.

"You right, girl. That's you. You should get that"

I capped. Miss, do you have any maternity clothes?" I asked, poking out my belly.

"Of course, we do?" The woman rushed over to me and guided me to the maternity section. She was all smiles.

Over my shoulder, I watched Peaches wrap some blouses around her waist and tuck the ends down the front of her blue jeans. "Ooohh…look at all this," I crooned to the woman, pointing. My job is to keep her eyes away from the others.

"Yes. We have so many, many selections for new mothers," she said obligingly.

"Excuse me, lady. Can I have this in an eighteen?" Peaches called to the woman again, spinning the woman toward her.

"Certainly."

Back and forth we spun the woman until we had all taken our share of merchandise and held an item apiece to take to the counter.

At the counter, Peaches asked, "How much do I need to put on this to keep it on lay-away?"

"Lay-away?" asked the woman.

"Yeah. Lay-away. How much?"

Disappointment crossed the woman's face. "Oh! I'm sorry. We don't do that."

"Whaaat?" sighed Celeste.

"You mean to tell me that I went through all this and ya'll don't lay-away?" argued Peaches.

"I'm so sorry. I was under the impression that you all knew." She pointed to the "No Lay-Away" sign posted behind her.

I tsked like I was soooo disappointed. "I'm outta here," I announced, leaving my outfit on the counter.

Peaches and Celeste followed.

Outside, we laughed and congratulated ourselves all the way out of the plaza's lot. That poor woman never stood a chance.

We stopped at a corner store for a bag to fill with our heist. Nine items we had boosted, all in the price range of forty to ninety dollars. I made it known that I was forfeiting some of my cut in order to keep a children's dress I'd stuffed for my eleven-year-old sister, Connie.

We sold the items, half-priced, to Celeste's aunt, a former Black Panther and now, a huge weed distributor to the neighborhood dealers. After another blunt and the lowering of the sun, I headed home, picked up a beef yok and four shrimp rolls on the way. There was no food when I left the house this morning, and I was almost certain there would be none when I got back.

I've lived in the Richard Allen projects all of my life. In the same house, in the center of the same row, on the same square, under the same conditions. Our two-bedroom tenement was on the second floor of a two-story row of homes that had little identity of their own. Each unit's exterior has its worn, peeling, burgundy and gray. The winter-green doors have deteriorated so much that their scars and scrapes were the only identification to tell whose house is whose. Some paint and scrubbing would camouflage the exteriors some, but graffiti artists will only see a new opportunity and Housing Authority just doesn't see the purpose in restoration if mind-sets haven't changed in decades.

Just when I closed the apartment door, Connie came running out of the bedroom.

"Mommy's drunk again," she whispered.

"Where she at?" I asked.

"In her room. Some man in there, too."

"Here. Take this." I gave Connie the food and watched her sift through the bag until she reached the living room sofa. She cleared a section of the small coffee table and set up shop.

"How long they been in there?" I asked.

"Wot wong?" Connie mouthed around a shrimp roll.

I made my way to the sofa and watched my sister eat like a misplaced refugee. Her complexion isn't as light as mine, but our mouths and noses are similar. She's a frail girl and, I feel bad for her having to grow up in the slums. "Did you eat at all today?" I asked dryly.

She nodded. "Danielle's mom made spaghetti and hotdogs. I didn't want no spaghetti, so I just ate hotdogs."

"You need to eat all you can." I lifted one of her thin arms. "Look how skinny you are."

She tsked. "So…if you wasn't pregnant, you be skinny, too."

I reached for a shrimp roll then remembered the dress

I had gotten her. I pulled the bag between us; "Here."

"What's that?"

"Look and see. Dang."

She reached for the bag.

I grabbed her wrist. "Uh-uh. Wipe your greasy hands first."

Connie scrambled for some tissue from the food bag then dove into the bag containing the dress. She pulled it halfway out, frowned then let it drop back inside. "Thanks," she grumbled.

"Damn, Ungrateful," I said.

"I said, 'thanks'."

"But like that?"

"Don't nobody wear no dresses no more."

"You will," I assured her.

"Uh-uhn."

"Yes. You will."

"Why I gotta wear a dress?"

"Because girls wear dresses."

"You don't wear 'em."

"That's not because I won't."

"Well, I'm not wearin' it to school." She picked at a roll.

"Why not?"

"'Cause at school, boys be tryna look under it."

She had a point. Even in high school, guys play those games with the girls who wear dresses and skirts.

"Guys are dogs," Connie said.

I thought about Hasim. "Did Hasim come pass?" I asked.

She shrugged. "I was over Danielle's."

I rested my head back, began rubbing my hands over my belly. I couldn't believe how big it's grown. For the first time, I noticed the 13" black and white TV was on. Grip pliers extended from the bottom channel turner. A clothes hanger made do for an antenna and Ricky Lake was on with

the volume turned down. I breathed deeply and closed my eyes. When I re-opened them, my mother was swaying before me, waving a shrimp roll in my face. I hadn't even realized I'd dosed off.

"If your ass wanna sleep, take your pregnant-ass in the room. I got company."

My eyelids fluttered as I tried to fully awaken myself.

I sat up and eyed my mother. "Why you waving that thing in my face?" I asked.

"Because…" She snatched a huge bite of the shrimp roll. "Your ass…" chew "don't…" chew "respect my company."

"You drunk," I simply said before standing.

"Ain't no mutherfuckin body drunk either." Her five-four frame swayed while she spoke. Her high yells skin is blemished from years of drug abuse and misused mascara. Crow's feet rested on the skin surrounding her glassy, brown eyes. She was all up in my face, and I could smell the vodka reeking off her.

"Can you, please, get outta my face, Mom?" I looked around for Connie who was nowhere in sight.

"Get outta your face, huh? Now you want me outta your face?" She backed up a few feet and pointed the half-eaten shrimp roll at me. "Maybe, if I was in your fuckin' face, your stank-ass wouldn't be all knocked up?" She snatched another bite of the roll. "Little bitch. Think you grown up, don't you?"

As much as I'd like to pop her just once, I knew I couldn't. She was still my mother, drunk or not. Plus, I needed a place to live, wanted to be there for Connie. "You drunk," I again said then turned and left.

"Bitch! Don't walk away from me!"

I was already gone, left her standing in the living room and slammed my bedroom door shut.

Connie was seated on the bed, crying. All I could think to do is stand there and watch her. On the other side of the door, my mother continued with her tirade, calling me all kinds of bitches and whores.

"I hate it here!" Connie yelled. "I thought you said we was leaving?"

"We will."

I tried to sound re-assuring, but I hadn't a clue where we would go. I buckled and leaned against the door. My baby was fighting to come out into this world. I wondered why.

CHAPTER 5

WESLEY

Bags and boxes layer the back seat of Stacks' brand-new Navigator. We were cruising through the pitted streets of North Philly after having gone shopping for tuxedoes for the wedding. Ludacris was blaring from the car's speakers. I surveyed Stacks at the wheel and smiled. He shows off when he drives, leans to the side, elbow resting on the armrest and with one wrist free to steer, bobs his head to the music.

As we turned onto Diamond from 24th Street then passed William Dick Elementary, a flood of memories bumrushed me, caused my insides to shrivel like wet noodles. I fought for breaths up until we passed Hank Gathers' Community Center on our way across the bridge toward 32nd Street.

Stacks parked the Navigator in front of the house where my uncle, Magic, now sub-leases from and shut down the engine. "Watch. Magic gonna trip when he see you."

I smiled at the idea of seeing Magic again. "Is he home?"

"Hell yeah. That fool home. He don't go nowhere but to work and the go-go clubs. Come on."

Norris Street looks to be crumbling at all phases. Dilapidated homes, broken and uneven sidewalks infested with brown weeds towering from between cement cracks. The street was beat down, like a losing fighter after the fifteenth round of a classic championship fights. I thought back to the gang-wars that had gone down on the street, just for the sake of claiming Norris Street. I wondered if ghosts of dead gangbangers were conforming a hood they'd like to see look more like hell. "You sure Magic here?" I asked Stacks. "I don't see his car."

"He's here. Probably got company. Yo, you gonna trip when you see the crib," Stacks knocked then banged twice more.

I saw the cream shade in the window move and heard Magic's cussing even before the chain was dropped from the door.

Magic met Stacks with a scowl. "Why you just don't ring the damn bell, boy?" he spat. He noticed me and grinned. "Get on in here, Wesley. How you doin'?"

We embraced.

I stepped by Magic and into the living room. I thought I'd stumbled onto the set of a 70's show. Magic had transformed the place into a bachelor pad layered with exotic fur rugs, wall to ceiling mirrors, and black leather. A collage of color burst from one corner where a pile of red, blue, and yellow throw pillows lie stacked.

I stood center-floor. "Damn, Magic, you doing some big pimpin up in here, huh?"

"You like?"

I laughed. "Cut it out, Unc. You know the old school theme ain't my twist."

"That's why you young-bucks don't know what time it is. Chicks dig this kinda set up."

Stacks plopped down on the leather sofa.

"Boy, take it easy!" Magic barked.

I chuckled.

"Don't worry, Unc, one lump won't change shit in here," said Stacks.

Magic pointed a warning finger at him. "I done tol' you 'bout sassin me, ain't I?"

"My bad, my bad," said Stacks.

Magic slowly turned back to me.

I took a seat across from Stacks in a large black recliner.

I've kept in touch with Magic since moving and knew he was playing the field since he and Gloria, his wife, had separated. I scanned the changes he'd made to the place. "So, you've changed my spot into a playa's pad, huh?"

He flagged me. "Aw, it'll do. Now, how come you just gettin back in town? You supposed to been back last week."

"Pam had his ass on lock down," Stacks said.

I shot a daggered stare at Stacks. "Two meetings came up. I had to be there."

Magic nods while deliberating. His George Jefferson hairline and shiny scalp slowly bounced.

"How's Gloria?" I asked.

"We still working things out. Sorta."

I gave him my yeah-right look, "It's been six years. How much working out do you need to work out?"

"It ain't her. It's me."

Stacks tossed a red throw pillow at me. I caught it.

"Magic thinks he's a playa, Wes. He be all up in this joint pimpin."

"Don't tell me that suave' mess he was kickin over the phone is true?"

"You better know it," said Magic with a cigarette-stained smile.

"You still at the garage, right?"

"Yep. Still there. I don't think much 'bout workin' for nobody else after being my own boss so long. Plus, Gloria ain't got nobody else to run the place. It's either me or sell the place…and she ain't doin that. She say when she dead, she'll give it up."

"Old as she is, that won't be long," added Stacks.

I threw the pillow back at him. Some things never change. Stacks still says the dumbest, disrespectful shit out of his face. "You need to be quiet sometimes," I told him.

"Hell, don't pay that ignorant fool no mind, Wesley. That woman of his'll straighten his behind out soon."

Magic and I gave each other daps.

Stacks smirked.

My eyes roamed the living room. I recalled some of my good and bad times in the house. What stuck out most was my last few weeks, memories of Carol and our last few nights together, nights of passion that had become the catapulting events which led to my decision to leave Philly. If only she hadn't found the clippings of Kevin's accident and the money I'd saved at the bottom of my closet. Maybe then, she and I would be living in the house, raising children, and possibly married. I can't help but think of her often, and since arriving in Philly, her image continuously keeps massaging my mind.

"Yo, dawg, you cool?" asked Stacks.

"What?"

"You all right?"

"Yeah. I'm straight. I was reminiscing…being back in this crib and all."

"Yeah, well, it's mine now," declared Magic. "You gave it up."

I took another look around. "Don't worry. The way you jacked it up, I don't think I could undo the damage."

Stacks and I laughed.

"Jacked up?" Magic began pointing at things. "You don't know nuttin 'bout coordinatin'."

I stood and flagged him. "Yeah. Okay, Unc."

Two hours passed before Stacks and I climbed back in the Navigator. The sound system was leveled just beneath our conversation. Jay-Z's "Song Cry" must've had Stacks thinking, because he opened up and started asking me questions about marriage — like I'd been married before. "I wish I knew," I answered for the second time.

"They say when you put that ring on their finger, they change." He shifted in the driver seat. "But I can't see that happening' wit' me and Big Girl. She know a niggah's style and she wit' it. You know what I mean, Wes?"

I nodded. "I hear you, bro."

"I mean…we got somethin' special goin', and I can't see how shit can change is all I'm sayin'."

"I hear you, bro."

We sat quiet a moment.

"Fuck that! I'm doin' this shit!" Stacks spat as if he'd made up his mind. "Then again…what if that shit true, Wes?"

"I hear you, bro."

I could tell from Stacks' strained expression that the reality of him getting married was puzzling for him. I have to admit to enjoying his torturing of himself, but as his best man, I feel obligated to step in and help out. I knew he was just having cold feet. "Stacks, listen…all that mess you hear and read out of those magazines, don't listen to. You and Sheila been living together for six years already. Everything you need to know about her, you already know. There are no secrets between you two. You've already seen her at her worst, and she damn sure seen you at yours. I've been telling you for years to stop reading that crap in those mags."

"Some 'a that shit be true," he said. He turned onto Diamond and flipped down the sun-visor to shield the sun's beams. A photo of Sheila was taped to the back, made me wish I wholeheartedly loved someone, too, made me think of Pam and our settling relationship.

"You know Big Girl's mom can't stand my guts, right?"

"Get outta here."

He nodded, extracted the CD, and put in a cassette tape. "Check this right here," he said while fidgeting with the stereo's equalizer. When the tape began, a thumping that made my heartbeat skip roared from the speakers. A voice as raw and raspy as Jarule filled the truck with poetic rhymes. After a couple of minutes of bouncing to beats, Stacks turned down the volume.

"Dope ain't it?" he asked.

"Who is that?"

"That's me right there."

I've heard Stacks rap before, and no way was that him. "Come on…that ain't hardly you rapping."

"Not rappin', fool. Producing. That's my first group, Maj or Bling."

"You joking?"

"Nope. I ain't jokin'. I'm tryna come up in the music biz."

I smiled. It felt good to know that Stacks was venturing into another game besides the "drug game". It was also Benny's dream to enter the record industry.

"Ay, man, I wish you all the success possibly."

We shook hands the Black man's way.

"And when your ass blow up like Puffy or JD, don't be frontin' on a brotha," I joked.

"Never that."

We stopped at a red light and sat quiet.

"Fuck that!" Stacks blurted. "I don't care if her mom's ain't feelin' me. We doin' this."

Stacks pulled off.

I laughed.

Sheila had outdone herself preparing dinner for my first day back in Philly. My plate was piled with food, a plate I've been dipping into since taking my place at the table. Spread across the table were huge bowls of golden, fried chicken, brown and white rice, buttered rolls, steamed string beans, and potato salad. Sheila had prepared a huge pumpkin pie covered with whip cream and assorted nuts sprinkled around its rim. At the rate that I was eating, I wasn't sure if I'd make it to dessert. Every few bites, Sheila rose to my side to pile on more. I couldn't believe how active she was. One might think that once she took her seat at the dinner table, she wouldn't want to be disturbed. Uh-uh. She was active and cute, too. A round face held a beautiful smile. I could clearly see her happiness in sparkling brown eyes. Her permed black hair hung to her small, double chin and hid some of the roundness of her face.

"Are you sure you have enough?" Sheila asked me.

"Positive."

"He don't know good eatin' no more, bay," remarked Stacks.

"Oh, I know good eating. Down South is where they really burn. You name it, they cook it. One day you might be petting some animal and, that night, you might find yourself chewing it."

"Ill. That's disgusting," Sheila crooned.

"You'd be surprised how good some of that stuff be tasting," I said. "It's all in how you hook it up, and sistahs down there can cook up a storm."

"Is that why people down South live to be a hundred?" Stacks asked.

"I don't know about all that." I bit into a huge chicken breast and savored the honey and light garlic flavoring.

"What about Pam? Can she throw down in the kitchen?" asked Sheila.

I shook my head and finished chewing. "Nope. Pam stays far away from the kitchen. We usually eat out or order in."

"That's a shame," coddled Sheila. She stood and started piling more string beans on my plate. "That's why I cook for my boo. A man should eat well." She tried throwing Stacks a satisfied smile on the way back to her seat, but Stacks hadn't lifted his head from his plate to acknowledge her. He was busy displaying why he'd picked up so much weight. Sheila had found the path to his heart.

After dinner, Sheila attended to the kitchen while Stacks and I were lounging in the living room, sipping Old English from cans. We were reminiscing about the share of dirt we'd done on the streets. Some things we'll never be able to rectify or make amends for. I had caught on to the destruction we had participated in way before Stacks, but now, I'm elated that he'd finally caught on. It had taken long enough. After Benny had been gunned down, I was unsure if Stacks or myself, to be honest, would ever be able to live down Benny's murder; and, now that Stacks is about to be married, I'm convinced that he's finally moved on in life. "You come around really good," I said to my brother.

"I had no choice," he replied.

"We always have choices. What we choose is something altogether different.

"Nah, Wes, I mean it. I got no choice. I'ma be a dad soon."

"What?"

A huge grin sprang to Stacks' face. "Yeah, bro, I'm about to be a pop, and you 'bout to be a uncle."

"Oh, snap! Congratufuckinlations!" I nearly ran over to shake his hand, but we embrace instead.

"When?" I asked.

"Big Girl's already two months."

"That's wonderful, bro. I'm happy for ya'll."

"Thanks, Yo."

We both were silent.

I sat back down.

"I'm glad you here, Wes. I missed you."

"I missed you, too, Lil bro. Now, where do I sleep? I gotta get you to your wedding rehearsal tomorrow."

CHAPTER 6

CAROL

Unlike the last time, James was at Janice's house when I brought the twins to visit with their grandmother. I had given serious thought to not letting them visit James after receiving his phone call. But, since the girls are old enough to understand what the situation is with their father, I let them make up their own minds — hence, we're all here, in Janice's living room.

Kevin and James' father were at the computer engrossed in a game of high-tech chess. Kevin has to be losing. He keeps hollering out, "Aw, Man!"

James was across the room, in a Lazy-Boy, rocking, eyeing me as if everything that has happened between us is my fault. I'd given him numerous choices and so many opportunities to remain a part of our lives, but he'd chosen his cocaine addiction instead. Now, regret was written on James' burnt-chocolate face.

Janice entered the living room pinching the sticks of two homemade apple taffies.

"Here you go, girls. I don't wanna see no mess around this house while ya'll eat these either."

Kia and Kelly leaped at her call. Both accepted a taffy from Janice's fingers.

"Thank you, Grandma," Kia said.

"And Kelly…?" Janice inquired.

"Thank you, Grandmom."

"You welcomed, Sugah."

"Where's mine?" I asked.

"You better get your butt in that kitchen and get one outta that freezer. My ankles 'bout to explode." She eased onto the sofa beside me, panting as if the task had robbed her of every ounce of energy. "Move over, chile."

"Aww, poor gramps," I teased.

Janice rolled her eyes. "Kia, honey, get a napkin from the roll over the kitchen sink 'fore you have that mess down your blouse."

Kia dropped the PlayStation remote and rose with a scowl. "Carol, I swear them girls sprouting like pumpkins."

"Don't I know it. I think I'm just gonna buy them bigger bras. I swear I can't keep up no more." I reached for Janice's hand and held it in mine. She's been a wonderful grandmother and mother-in-law, although James and I had never married. "Have you been taking your medicine?" I asked.

"Not now, chile, please?"

"No. She ain't took a thing," James answered.

"Hush, man. Ain't nobody asked you nothing."

"Well, you haven't," refuted James.

"And it ain't nobody business but my own. I'm the one gotta deal with it."

It's been difficult to watch Janice have to deal with the pain of living with breast cancer. Ever since finding out, she's let herself go, has lost more than sixty pounds in a year.

"Why don't you come to the church with Kevin and me?" I asked Janice.

"Now, Carol, you know I love the Lord, but I ain't about to be no hypocrite."

"You won't be a hypocrite. All we're doing is helping out."

"I still don't wanna go."

I patted her hand and stood. "Well, we have to. I'll pick the girls up on my way home, okay?"

"Mm-hm. I hear you."

"Come on, Janice. Don't be this way."

"What way? Honey go on and do whatever it is you have to do. Never mind me."

I stared down at Janice, heavy-hearted. When I had been pregnant with Kevin, Janice took me into her home and cared for me like I was her own. But, over the six years that James and I have been apart, I barely visit, mostly because of school, but there's my not wanting to see James' face. He's been living with Janice for the past two years. I kissed Janice's cheek. "Love you," I whispered.

"Mm-hm," she hummed.

"Behave yourselves," I warned the twins. Neither paused from PlayStation or acknowledged my leaving. "Kevin, you ready?"

"One second, Mom."

"Well, hurry, please?"

"I need to talk to you, Carol," said James, raising from the Lazy-Boy. He's been quiet throughout most of my visit, so I wasn't surprised he wants to talk.

"About what, James?" I asked.

"Can we talk in private?"

"You can walk me to the car, because I gotta go." I turned to Kevin. "Boy, would you come on?"

"I'm coming. Hold up, Mom."

Outside, cloaked beneath a paucity of white clouds amidst the mid-afternoon's heat, Richard Island project's large courtyard was buzzing with activity. Children were hollering and giggling while riding bicycles across the blacktop while some little girls sang modern folk rhymes while skipping double-Dutch. The older residents, perched on steps, sipped on iced beverages. The adults looked on at over-developed teens clad in short sets and belly-shirts that displayed their many shades of brown skin. Kevin had wheeled himself over to the car. James and I were standing on the steps of Janice's rowhome.

"Thanks for bringing the girls by," James said.

"It was their decision, not mine. If it were my decision, they wouldn't be here for nobody except your mom."

Disappointment covered his face. "How long you gonna make me pay for the past?"

"I'm not asking you to pay for anything, James. You made your choice. Live with it."

"I made the wrong choice. I know you see my regret."

I peered into his coal-black eyes and breathed deeply to let him know I'd heard it all before. "I gotta go, James. Is that all?"

"No. Not exactly."

"Then what?"

"I'm workin' again, and I wanted to give you this." He pulled a roll of bills from his pocket and held them out to me.

"What's that?"

"Somethin' for the girls. I know it's been a while so…"

"We're fine, James."

His arm fell to his side. "Oh, my money ain't good enough no more?"

"That's not it."

"Then what?"

"It's just that…well…you need it more than us. We're fine. I know you're still getting on your feet with NA meetings and all…so, take your time. Get your own self together."

"That's just it. Giving you this money is part of my rehab. My selfishness is what got us here. So, please, take the money?"

I huffed. "Give me the money then, James."

The last thing I wanted was child support from James. To me, his giving the money will only leave an impression that all is forgiven between us and that his full parental rights have unofficially been reinstated -- and they haven't. Over the years, I've been so disgusted with James that I could barely stomach seeing him.

I dropped the bills in my purse and wanted to slap the smug look from his face. Of course, I wanted to see James get himself together, but not at the expense of my own convictions. I'd made a pact with myself, after he'd walked out on us, to raise my children on my own. He'd abused me enough.

"Let me help you with Kevin's chair," he offered. He was already heading for the car before I could protest.

I could see the displeasure on Kevin's face. He despises what James had done to us probably more than I do.

Before the chair was in the trunk, I had the car started and in "Drive". When the trunk closed, I pressed the gas and took off, waved goodbye to James' pursed lips from the rearview. I smiled then noticed Kevin's smirk. "What are you looking at?" I asked Kevin.

He shook his head.

"What?" I asked.

"You know what."

"No. I don't. Why don't you tell me?"

"He sweatin' you now."

I turned the car out of the courtyard and onto 11th Street. "That don't mean I'm going to give into him."

"I hope not. He dogged you."

"Shut up, Kevin."

"You know I'm telling the truth."

I concentrated on my driving, not wanting to admit that my son was right. James had dogged me, left me to raise my children alone and had given me his black behind to kiss. All from drugs. Now that I'd gotten used to doing without him, he's been trying to reinsert himself into our lives. Well, Daddy's Little Girls may not be thick-skinned enough to deflect all of James' bull, but I'd been groomed by a different set of circumstances which I hope neither of my daughters will ever have to live through.

Mission Baptist Church was a few minutes' drive from Janice's house and just long enough drive to refocus my thoughts from James. I helped Kevin into his chair and wheeled him to the church's ramp. Pastor Riley was there to greet us. She looked tiny in her large, blue choir robe with one thick, white stripe running from neck to hem.

"I'm glad you made it, Sister Shavers. I was hoping you would. Hello, Kevin." She kissed Kevin's cheek.

"I was running late," I said.

She flagged my excuse. "Just as long as you're here."

We followed her inside of the church.

"As you can see, we've been decorating," said Pastor Riley.

"I can tell," I mused.

An array of bouquets decorated the foyer.

"We're preparing for a wedding ceremony this weekend that I'm looking forward to. It's a good thing you're here. I can use your help unloading boxes."

Near the entrance were several cardboard boxes. Layering their tops were white laced materials, candles, and plastic greenery.

"Well, I guess we better get to it then," I replied. I noticed others, near the pews, with their backs to us.

"Kevin, you come with me. I have the perfect thing for you to do," said the pastor. She nudged me from behind the chair and whisked Kevin away. "Just bring the decorations in here, Sister Shavers, and set them near the back pew."

I adjusted my purse's strap. "Sure," I mumbled before collecting the first box. I was surprised how light it was. I grabbed the corner of another and dragged it along, too. I could barely see what was ahead of me, but managed to get to the pew safely. I was stacking one box on top of another when a man's voice rang from behind me.

"Hello, Carol." The voice sounded familiar. Baritone.

Shocking.

I spun around and the box slipped from my fingers and crashed to the floor. Its contents spewed across the red carpet.

My heartbeat skipped. "Wesley," I mumbled.

"Yeah, it's me."

Beside Wesley was Kevin, brandishing a wide grin. "What? Why?…What are you doing here?" I stammered.

"His brother's getting married," Kevin answered.

"Married?" My eyes never wavered from Wesley's. My voice was hard to pull from my throat.

"Yes. My brother, Stacks, is getting married this weekend. This is his rehearsal."

I kneeled and began collecting items from the floor. Wesley's face appeared next to mine as he helped. His eyes searched my face. I didn't know whether to scream or scratch out his eyes.

"It's good to see you again," he said.

I hadn't realized how hard I was slamming the decorations back into the box until Kevin interrupted.

"Mom, what's wrong?"

"Nothing." I was trying to avoid both of their eyes. My thoughts were in the past, six years ago, when I had discovered that Wesley was responsible for accidentally shooting Kevin during a drug war. When I did find out that Wesley had been involved, it had been too late. We were already lovers. Both of us had been creeping.

"How have you been?" asked Wesley.

"Fine. Simply fine." I continued snatching items and slamming them into the box.

"How long you staying?" Kevin asked Wesley. "Mom said you moved to Atlanta somewhere."

"Yep. I'll be here for a week." Wesley eyed me as if he needed my permission to stay in town.

I stood, brushed the knees of my jeans while wishing Kevin would shut up; although, I found myself somewhat curious. I already knew that Wesley had transformed his life after the incident, had left the drug life and graduated from Temple University. For two years, Wesley had sent anonymous envelopes to Kevin filled with cash. His idea of retribution, I guess.

After our falling out, he had left town, had left a package containing fifty-thousand dollars in my mailbox. He'd also left me broken-hearted. He and James are the reasons I've been celibate all of these years.

"Let's go, Kevin. We have things to do," I said.

"Huh?"

"We're leaving."

Confusion rode Kevin's face. "Leave for what? We just got here."

"Don't argue with me, please? Let's just go."

"But Mom…Wes?" He was looking at Wesley for answers.

I noticed that Wesley's dreds had grown shoulder-length and I'd forgotten his eyes which were still that beautiful shade of hazel. I fought to erase the images from my mind of the intimate moments we'd shared. Instead, I focused on the wrong he had done by taking another person's life, the crippling of my son in the process. Seeing Wesley again mentally placed me back in Raymond Rosen projects and back on welfare.

"You should listen to your mom, Kevin," he said. It infuriated me that he would counsel my son.

Pastor Riley joined us and handed me a box of black plastic alphabets. "Sister Shavers, when you're done moving the boxes, would you mind terribly if I had you prepare the billboard out front of the church and the one in the foyer?"

I had forgotten all about the boxes or even volunteering. Before I could answer, Pastor Riley was wheeling Kevin away again. "Kevin, you can aide me with the ceremonious decorations," she was saying.

I felt trapped standing alone with Wesley, forced to relive the hurt and anger I had felt when I discovered Wesley's deceit. "Please, Carol. It's been six years of agony for me. Can we at least talk?"

I shifted my weight to my back foot and felt the hairs at the base of my neck stand up. Everyone suddenly wants to talk. "And what exactly do you think we have to talk about?"

"How sorry I am."

"You already said that. Anything else?" I stared daggers at him.

"I know you're hurt, Carol, but neither of us can change what happened. I'm willing to do anything, anything to make amends. All you have to do is say it."

"I don't want to talk to you," I simply said. My eyes roamed the rehearsal.

Across the room, Kevin was cutting his eyes toward us while folding napkins. He was obviously wondering why I'm so upset with Wesley. The last thing I want is to hurt Kevin by telling him that Wesley's responsible for crippling him. He'd taken a liking to Wesley since their first meeting. I tried to make our conversation appear casual, but venom still dripped from my words. "Wesley, you lied to me, deceived me, used me. Not only did you use me, but you used Kevin."

"But, Carol, I didn't —"

"Don't 'but Carol' me," I snarled. "You did!"

Our voices had begun to carry, and eyes were wandering in our direction. I felt a need to keep our secret quiet. I didn't know if it was ' because I'd made love to Wesley or had used some of the money he'd left behind to put myself through school. Or was it the guilt of loving and yearning for him — even after finding out who he was and what he'd done? He's been an after-thought in my life for six years now. Because of Wesley, so much of my life has been altered.

Pastor Riley eased beside us. "Is everything all right here?"

Wesley looked away just as I did. "Everything's fine," I answered then walked off.

When I returned, dragging two more boxes, Wesley was with the wedding party of six. I went to attend to the billboards. When I was done the boards, Wesley and Kevin were near the alter, conversating. Kevin saw me and headed my way. I was thankful, too, because I was ready to leave.

I explained to Pastor Riley that I wasn't feeling particularly well and needed to leave earlier than expected.

She kissed my cheek and said that everything will be okay, "It's all in God's hands," she added.

Kevin and I were in the car, headed back to Janice's house to pick up the twins. Kevin was continuous with his beatbox noises, pushed me closer to a migraine. "Kevin can you, please, stop that?" I braked at a red light and rested my head back.

"You okay, Mom?"

I nodded.

"Can I ask you something then?"

"What?" I answered, pulling away at the green light. "What's up with you and Wes?"

"Nothing."

"I saw ya'll arguing about something."

"It's nothing, Kevin." Even as I told the lie, I recalled the passion Wesley and I had shared.

"Wes says he'll give me a job after I graduate — if I need one."

"He did, huh?"

"Yup. He gave me his business card. See…" Kevin pulled out the card and fingered it toward me.

I cut my eyes toward it, saw Kevin's smiling face.

"You can find your own job, Kevin. Don't be depending on people to give you anything." I turned onto 11th Street and paused at a "STOP" sign.

"I'm not depending on it. It's good that he offered is all I'm saying. Dag. What's wrong with you? You act like you hate him all of a sudden."

"I don't hate anyone."

"Well, I know you used to like him before he moved. Even at the church you acted like you wanted to get away from him."

"Kevin, just be quiet, please? You don't have the slightest idea what you're talking about."

"I know a love jones when I see one," he said, raising his arms to protect from a possible blow.

I kept my hands on the steering wheel and wondered if I were indeed still in love with Wesley.

CHAPTER 7

FELICIA

Before I entered my sixth period classroom, Mrs. Wright, my math teacher, stopped me at the door.

"Miss Knight, you're wanted at the guidance counselor's office." She handed me a hall pass and nodded for me to go on.

Being summoned to the counselor's office used to be routine for me. Before Mrs. Spellman decided to retire, we used to have long talks about all kinds of things, but now that she's no longer at the school… I'm not about to confide in someone else.

I reached the counselor's office and knocked, hoped this woman hadn't called me to discuss the confrontation we had in the bathroom. Through the school's grapevine, I had found out just who the woman from the bathroom was.

"Come in," a voice called.

I entered the small office with my gas-face on. She was at her desk, shuffling though folders.

"I was told to come here."

A smile spread her lips. "I know. I asked that you be excused from the class. You don't mind, do you?"

I shook my head. "Whatever."

"Good. I think we should talk. Come in and have a seat." She pointed to a chair beside her desk.

I chose the leather chair directly across from her instead. She continued smiling.

I set my book-bag on the floor beside me.

"I wanted to speak with you, Felicia, about your intentions when your child is born."

"Intentions? What kinda intentions?"

"School. Work. How you intend on raising your child. Its father. Basic stuff."

I breathed deeply and prepared myself for the lecture I'd avoided in the bathroom.

"You don't want to hear this, do you?" she asked.

"No."

"Neither did I."

"Huh?"

"Neither did I. The last thing I wanted to hear, when I was pregnant at thirteen, was what adults thought."

I tsked. "Yeah right. You was pregnant at thirteen?"

She nodded, stacked some folders on top of one another and pushed them to one side of her desk. She folded her fingers on the desk, studious-like, and gave an understanding smile. "That's why I wanted to speak with you. We have a lot in common."

"Being pregnant young don't make us have a lot in common," I shot back.

"True. But there's more. For starters, I grew up in a foster home and spent most of my life in the projects."

"You lying," I challenged.

"One thing I won't do is lie to you, Felicia."

I rubbed my belly and searched for a reason to get up and leave. Nobody has got it worse than me. Nobody! I thought. "I guess you gonna tell me that your mother's a drunk, too?" I asked.

"No. Because then I'll have to tell you that I knew her, and I never did."

I gazed down at my lap and imagined never knowing my mother.

For as long as I can remember, my mother's been a drunk and a stripper. Not knowing her might've made life so much easier. "Okay…say we do have some things in common…what do you want from me?"

"I told you. To know your intentions. I know I had no clue what to do with a baby. Do you?"

I sat speechless, unable to answer her question, not because I had no answer to give, but because I knew that my answer would embarrass me. "I know what to do," I replied.

She grinned.

"What?" I asked.

"Nothing. It's just that I said the same thing."

"You think you know me, don't you?"

She raised trimmed eyebrows and nodded.

Miss Shavers had tossed every stereotype I'd perceived of her right out of the window. This can't be the same woman from the bathroom, I thought. My shields lowered.

"Honestly, I don't know how I'ma raise my baby, but it'll have everything it need."

"What about the father?" she asked. "Do you think you'll be able to depend on his help?"

I shrugged. "If he ain't in jail or dead." Suddenly the thought of Hasim changing diapers saddened me. I knew that I could depend on

Hasim for financial support, but I also knew that his support could end with the clicking of handcuffs.

"There are child services available if you'd like to take advantage of some of them." She reached into her drawer and handed me several pamphlets. "How are things at home?"

"Hectic."

"I'm sorry to hear that. I was reading through your file and noticed there's no mention of your father. I assume you aren't close?"

"It's just me, my mom, and my sister. I never met my dad."

Miss Shavers and I spoke until the bell rang for next period. She seemed pretty down to earth, kind of cool really. I left her office high-spirited, with the impression that she's really concerned about where I'm headed in life. She even gave her number — just in case. I had tucked the number in my pants pocket, and now it feels like the slip of paper was branding my thigh. I wasn't sure if I'd ever need it but decided to keep it anyway — just in case.

Celeste and Peaches met me at my school locker shortly after the final bell. Celeste was excited because Rhonda, her eye-candy, had finally shown her some attention. Celeste can be kind of goofy at times, but overlooking that, she's someone you'd want in your corner.

Peaches was watching Celeste through slanted eyes and probably thinking just what I was. "Celeste, wake up. Rhonda just wanna taste that thing and move right along," said Peaches.

Celeste gave Peaches the finger. "You just jealous 'cause nobody sweatin' your big ass that's all."

"You wish."

"I know. If they were those big ol' bloomers would'a been dropped, okay?" Celeste joked. She rolled her eyes from Peaches to me. "Girl, what did the GC say?"

I tossed my books in the locker and slammed the door shut. "She gave me some pamphlets and stuff that's all. I threw that mess in the trash," I lied, not wanting them to know that I didn't have my shit together.

"Did she say anything about smoking in the bathroom?" Celeste asked.

"Nope. She said she grew up in the projects and got pregnant young, too."

"Bitch probably lying," Peaches exclaimed. "She probably said all that to get you to spill your guts so that she can dissect your life and shit."

"I don't wanna talk about her," I said.

"I know that's right, 'cause Lil' Lee-Lee got two god moms right here to look out, okkaaayyy?"

I gave Peaches the high-five she was seeking as we headed towards the school's exit amidst the surge of other students filing from the doors.

After school is always an event. There's constantly some drama going on somewhere on the school grounds. You can almost count on it. What you couldn't count on is whether it'll be you that's involved in the drama taking place, and when I turned onto Broad Street, near the school's front exit, Hasim was standing there all up in some senior's face. She was obviously interested in what Hasim was saying. She was giggling, flirtatiously, with a hand in one of his.

We stopped walking, and I could feel Peaches and Celeste staring at me. "Oh, no the hell he ain't," I mumbled.

"He know he dead wrong," said Celeste, echoing my exact sentiments.

Before I reached the small group, Hasim saw me coming. His entire posture changed.

He'd been busted.

I wasn't about to embarrass myself in front of his boys, my girls or some skeezer, but my heart dropped to my feet. I began trembling and my hand paused at my belly as I took in both separating. Reaching the group, I pointed from one to the other. "What the hell is this?" I spat.

"Aw, it ain't nuttin. We just chillin," Hasim answered all nonchalant. "This here's Mona."

My eyes swept Mona's petite figure and sly smile before returning to Hasim. "I know she better be a sister that I don't know about…all up on you and shit."

"Come on, bay, don't start."

"Don't start?" I snapped then caught myself. "You come all up to my school with this bitch all draped around you."

"I ain't no bitch," Mona replied.

"Ho', ain't nobody talkin' to you," I snarled.

"Ho'?"

"That's what the fuck I said."

"Uh-uh. You better get your little friend," Mona told Hasim. Celeste and Peaches eased to my side.

I held up an arm to hold back the ass-whuppin I knew they would happily give to Mona.

"Chill. Damn," Hasim said. "Let me speak to you for a minute, bay."

We were off to the side of everyone else. Peaches and Celeste were still staring Mona down, who had draped her bookbag over her shoulder and began easing away. I was sure she sensed an ass-whuppin.

"Bay, ain't nuttin' to that chicken-head, okay? We was laughin' an' kickin it. That's all. She ain't got nuttin on you."

"Uh-uh, Hasim. You totally disrespectin' me."

"What?"

"Every time I turn around, you eyeballin' or flirtin' with some skank. You want them bitches go 'head."

He blushed. "Come on, boo, you buggin'."

"Buggin' shit! Just like I was buggin' when you snuck off with your ex, huh?"

"What?" He looked confused.

"Mm-hm. Thought I was sleep on that, too, huh?"

Hasim stepped back, speechless. "It ain't like that, bay."

"Then what's it like?"

Hasim stood there Hip-Hop to the bone. Tattoos. Baggy pants. Bandana. If only I could convince him that famous rappers don't really live like this. But that would be like explaining to a blind man the color red.

"Look…if you done lyin', Hasim, I just wanna get away from here." I spun on my heels and paused at the sight of Miss Shavers watching us. Somehow, I felt like I'd shattered her hopefulness. My eyes lingered at the ground. When I looked up, she was walking away.

Our after-school hangout is a McDonalds located a block away from William Penn high school. Hasim and I were sharing a booth with Cal and Tina while Peaches and Celeste stood arguing with a cashier about a too rare hamburger.

"So, what time do you think you'll be back?" I asked Hasim.

"'Bout eleven."

"Then I won't see you til' tomorrow?"

"Not unless your moms let me show through."

I knew that wasn't going to happen. Although Hasim's mother and mine had been friends, my mother resents the fact that Hasim has gotten me pregnant so young — Hasim being nineteen and all, and her expecting better from us both.

Cal and Trina snickered.

I shot them both a sneer that sent them attending to their burgers and fires. "Why can't we ever do something by ourselves — without anybody else around?" I asked Hasim as I motioned toward his friends.

"We do."

"No. We don't. It's always your boys around."

"Well, your girls always around."

"But I don't have a problem leaving them. You do."

"Well, a niggah gotta roll deep to keep suckers up offa me." He balled up his face. "Why you trippin'?"

Hasim's beeper went off, caused me to push my Big Mac to the center of the table.

He checked his beeper. "I gotta pick a little somethin' up in a few. You straight gettin' home?"

I nodded. "Go 'head, Hasim."

"Cool."

Cal rushed three huge bites from his sandwich then crumbled the wrapper.

It was obvious they had been waiting for the page and that I had been something in the meantime. All three of them slide from the booth.

Hasim pecked my cheek. "I'll see tomorrow, boo."

Again, I nodded.

After Hasim had left the restaurant, I sat there brooding until Peaches and Celeste sat with me. They had new sandwiches and worried eyes.

"You okay, girl?" Celeste asked.

"It's all good," I answered. "Let ' em do his thing."

Connie doesn't much care for McDonald's food, so I picked up turkey and cheese hoagies, a ninety-nine cents liter of Pepsi, and a family-size bag of B&Q chips for dinner. I've learned from past experiences not to come home with only two sandwiches, so to avoid hearing my mother's mouth, I got her one too.

Connie and I were at the kitchen table. She was explaining to me the new steps she and her drill team were practicing. Momma was in the living room, playing oldies, drunk as usual, but in a fairly good mood, nonetheless.

"Hand me the big jar?" I asked Connie.

"It's dirty."

"Then wash it out." I shook my head and watched her go to the sink. She kept rambling on about the drill team.

From the living room, Momma's crooning of the Stylistics' "You Are Everything" could be heard.

Connie sat the cleaned jelly jar beside me while I filled it with Pepsi.

"Take that to Mom."

She tsked but did what I asked. I knew that she really didn't want to. She was ready to eat.

When she returned, almost skipping, I had already poured myself a cup of soda and was a bite into my sandwich. I'd left the half-emptied liter of soda for her. She loves drinking from the bottle. I think she picked that habit up from watching Momma drink.

"Did she say anything to you," I asked.

Connie shook her head while tearing open her sandwich. "She in there dancin' and stuff. She not gonna drink it. She gonna pour her vodka in it."

"Be quiet and eat."

She shrugged. "It's true."

And it is. Connie was right, but I didn't feel up to the truth right now. Every day, except for Momma's check day, I must bring home food. Occasionally, she'd spend half of the food stamps, welfare gives her, shopping for food, but mostly her speakeasy tab consumes the majority. Momma would rather drink than eat. Long ago, I got the message. She believes we'd rather fend for ourselves.

When Connie and I were through eating, we passed through the living room unnoticed by Momma, who had her eyes shut, cradling the jelly jar of booze and soda while swaying to Gerald Lavert. For the first time in a long while, I opened my English textbook and enjoyed doing my homework. I even went over some of Connie's division with her and felt the satisfaction of her catching on so quickly. I was surprised that because I've never fully committed to my schoolwork, I've managed to maintain C's and B's. I wondered just what I could do if I applied myself.

The following morning, I was running late. I met Celeste and Peaches at McDonalds. Celeste was tomboyishly dressed, clad in baggy jeans, short-sleeved rugby shirt, and a Phillies' baseball cap. Peaches, in jeans and a "All Hugs Come Here" Tee, was teasing her about her crush on Rhonda when I slid in the booth.

"Dang, Lisha, we was about to roll," Celeste said.

"Ya'll coulda left. I know my way."

"Excuuussee me," said Peaches, rolling her eyes. "You gettin' somethin' to eat or what?"

I shook my head. "Ya'll see Hasim?"

Both answered no.

I could tell from their expressions that their thoughts were as mine. Yesterday's confrontation with Mona.

"Girl, you better worry about that baby eatin'. Forget Hasim," Celeste said.

I knew she was right, so, on my way to school, I munched on an Egg McMuffin and a medium cup of orange juice. We stopped on a back street and the three of us shared a blunt. I was feeling nice and mellow when we entered the school, believed I would handle any situation I might be faced with, until I nearly bumped into Miss Shavers on my way to homeroom. Her eyes gave me the impression that she knew I was high. They were scolding.

"Hello, Felicia," she greeted.

"Hi," I giggled, trying to mask my mellow groove. It was useless. The weed had been good.

CHAPTER 8

WESLEY

Putting together a bachelor party for Stacks hadn't been as complicated as I thought it would be. Thrown together was a mixture of homies, strippers, and liquor and I was able to master the art of creating a festive atmosphere. Where to have the party had been an even easier task to tackle. I had rented a suite at the Bellevue on Locust, and none of the fifteen homies or eight female strippers seem to regret the provisions I've made.

With a backdrop of white walls and beige furniture, the men stood semi-circled, gawking at two strippers performing a lap dance on Stacks, who'd been set center-floor in a straight back chair. Sharissa's "Any Other Night" gave the strippers a slow rhythm that caused my mind to drift toward infidelity and Stacks' tongue to continuously run across his lips. Stacks was in a heavenly state of mind as were the homies who were being worked on by the remaining strippers. I was scanning the wide smiles, lustful glares, and bulged eyes when a stripper named Penny eased from behind me in one smooth seductive move.

"You enjoying yourself, baby?" Penny cooed.

I sipped the champagne I'd been nursing and gave a satisfied nod.

"That's good to know," she purred as she pressed her thronged buttocks against me and glared backward with slanted, lust-filled eyes. She seductively ran her pierced tongue across gold painted lips, bent to the floor, and wiggled her rump.

"Lordy, lordy, lordy," I gasped.

Up, down and around her booty toyed with me until I felt myself responding.

She must have felt it too, because she smiled knowingly and slithered on to the next man.

My attention turned back to Stacks, who was now shirtless and drooling.

Both strippers were topless and shaking at least thirty-eight D's while wiggling bronze, big-boned bodies — just the way Stacks likes.

"Aww, sooki-sooki now," Magic cried out when the two strippers began dancing with one another.

When they kissed, the entire room hummed with male enthusiasm. There wasn't a brother in the room who didn't want to be between the strippers' lip lock. Not one — including myself.

Later, after everyone had gone, and I had finished fighting to put Stacks' drunken butt to bed, I slid beneath a cold shower. Once revived from the champagne and long evening, I stepped out onto the suite's patio to take in the early morning skyline.

I'd missed being home, missed the city of Brotherly Love for too long. Regardless of how ugly I thought of the lifestyle I'd run away from, my heart still held the city's weight. The culture of the city is deeply embedded in me, its monuments, and roads are so far etched in my mind and soul that they're hopelessly impossible to erase. The South Streets. Art museum. Love Parks. Restaurants and Hotels. The air itself warrants its own memory of fresh bakeries lining the pavements of the industrial strips.

So much have I missed as I now look down onto the darkened, half-deserted streets I had once hustled on. The people themselves, whether they spoke a hello or stared cross-eyed while passing, was as much missed as anything else. Cheese steaks.

Hoagies. Mustard pretzels. The cab drivers, the shop keepers, the homeless, dingy, and balled upon weathered cardboard boxes layered throughout the city's subways.

Yes, I've missed the ghetto streets that I had once preyed on. However, it had been necessary to leave, and I understood that then. But now, as I breathed in the city's enticements, maybe, just maybe, I thought, I could have gotten through Benny's death without leaving my roots.

More unsettling thoughts entered my mind, thoughts of my past relationship with Carol and my responsibilities to Kevin for altering his young life. I shivered in the early morning air and wondered if having seen Carol again was healthy for me. seeing her has caused an explosion of emotions to linger within me. All that I had felt for her, six years ago, has resurfaced.

And ever since the wedding rehearsal, I haven't been able to shake Carol's image from my mind. For some people, time heals all wounds; but, from Carol's reaction to seeing me after six years, it was obvious that not enough time has gone by for her to forgive me for betraying her trust.

I left the early morning chill and settled on the sofa. I stared at the mess scattered across the suite. Empty liquor bottles. Overflowing ashtrays. Half-eaten sandwiches. Bowls of soiled party mixes. The pungent aroma of Philly blunts still lingered in the room. I had been tempted but hadn't taken a puff. I'd promised myself years ago to never indulge again. So far, I've kept that promise.

I grabbed the stereo remote and clicked on the CD player.

Maxwell's "Lifetime" filled the room. I sank into the sofa's velour cushioning, rested my head back, and closed my eyes. It hadn't taken me long to drift off to sleep.

When my eyes reopened, daylight was filtering through the window's blinds and my cellphone was ringing. I stumbled across the suite to my jacket pocket and snatched up the phone. "Yeah," I sleepily answered.

"Wes?" the voice asked.

"Yeah. Who's this?"

"Kevin."

I cleared my throat and strained my eyes fully open. "Kevin who?"

"You know…the guy in the wheelchair?"

"Yeah. I remember you now. What's up? How'd you get my number?"

"You gave it to me. Remember?"

"Oh. Yeah, I remember. So, what's up? Is everything okay?"

"Yeah. It's just that, uh…well…I got these tickets…and uhm…I thought you might wanna come to a Sixers' game with me."

"Me? A Sixers' game?"

"Yeah. Basketball. They got a team in Atlanta, right?" My head was still groggy.

"Uh…yeah, they got a team."

"So, you wanna come?"

"Yeah. Sure. Oh! What about your mom?"

"What about her?"

"Well, she uh…I don't think she — "

"Don't worry about Mom. I got this."

"Okay then. I'll pick you up."

"No. You don't have to do that. The game is at eight. I'll meet you at the First Union at seven. We can catch the shoot around."

"Cool. I'll see you at seven then." I pressed the phone's off button and wondered if I'd made the right decision. I couldn't very well turn Kevin down. I had told him to call me if he needed anything, and if it's a friend to go to the game with that he needs, then I wanted to be there for him.

The First Union Center is a multi-sports stadium where a diverse number of events are hosted, but mostly, it's home for Sixers and Flyers' games. Tonight, the Sixers are hosting an Eastern rival, the New York Knicks, and from the volume of traffic pulling into the parking areas, the game must have sold out of tickets.

I parked a good distance from the stadium's entrance and because of the heat, loathed the long walk it had taken to reach the building. I'd dressed casually. Jeans. Nikes. T-shirt. Already I've been posted against the huge white building for nearly twenty minutes, watching enthused Sixers' fans hurry into the stadium.

A few minutes later, I spotted Kevin being pushed across the stadium's parking area by no one other than Carol. I had no idea she'd be joining us, and my heartbeat quickened, made me consider hiding somewhere. But, from where I was positioned, I was sure Kevin had already noticed me, especially since he was expecting me to be there. Suddenly, the parking area didn't seem so large anymore. I wondered if there would be room for Carol's anger and my regret. I was sure the Sixers wouldn't be the only ones involved in a war tonight.

CHAPTER 9

CAROL

It had taken two days for my mind to feel at ease and my heart to stop fluttering whenever I'd run across a man wearing dreds. I'm not too surprised, though. After all, it had taken me two years to recover from Wesley, and now that I've seen him again, I would assume chat it's only natural that I experience some sort of emotional period. I clipped on the back of my gold-looped earring and shut the dresser drawer.

"Come on, Mom. We only got an hour!" Kevin called from downstairs.

"'We only got an hour,' I mimicked as I rushed to get myself ready.

There was a knock at the front door. "Mom, Aunt Tonya here!" Kevin yelled.

I heard the twins' footsteps charge from their room and down the stairs. "Stop running down those steps!" I yelled as I continued checking myself in the mirror. I had allowed my hair to grow shoulder length over the last few months, but prefer it pulled into a ponytail I added some eyeliner to my thin brows then headed downstairs.

I entered the living room to find Tonya twisting the loose end of one of Kia's braids.

"Hey, girl," I greeted her.

She hummed hello across the red barrette pressed between her thick lips. She pulled it from her lips. "Hold still, Kia. You should'a been had your hair together when I called and told ya'll I was on my way."

Tonya had offered to take the girls to the movies tonight while I go to the game with Kevin. She mugged Kia's head away from her when she was through.

Kevin and Kelly were busy on PlayStation.

"Here," I said to Tonya. I handed her a twenty-dollar bill. "If you feed them, it's on you."

"Stop being so cheap," she replied. "You lucky I'm even takin' these rug rats."

"You another one," replied Kelly from the PlayStation.

"Oh, no you didn't." Tonya rushed over and plucked Kelly's head. "Mom!" she yelled playfully without letting loose her remote or turning from the television. "Mom nothin'," Tonya said.

Kia ran over to help by smacking Tonya's big booty then running.

"Oh, ya'll gonna roll on me?" played Tonya.

"That's okay. I'ma leave ya'll butts right in the movies."

"I know my way home," Kelly said definitely.

Tonya balanced her pear-shaped body on one leg as if she knows karate. "Ya'll keep actin' like Aunt Tonya don't know her stuff, hear?"

I laughed and grabbed my keys from the table. "Tonya, sit your crazy-behind down before you tip over.

She turned to me. "You can get some' a this, too."

"Puh-lease, girl," I laughed.

Tonya is my foster sister — not of my last foster parents, who were Jehovah Witnesses, but of my foster parents before them. We had made a pact to always be there for one another.

"Kevin bring your butt on. You done rushed me to get ready."

"What time you want me to bring these knuckleheads home?" Tonya asked.

"You can keep 'em as far as I'm concerned."

"Honey. I can't even deal with' my own. That's why they daddy got 'em." She wasn't lying either, and she said it in all earnest.

Tonya had birthed two boys, who are now fifteen and seventeen, and still, at thirty-five, Tonya feels little obligation to raise either son. It's not as if she doesn't love them. I wouldn't go as far as to say that. She visits them regularly, buys them gifts, and does most motherly things — even scolds them at times. However, she just seems content on allowing her ex-lover, their father, to handle the bulk of the responsibility for them. She's a firm believer that boys should be with their dads and girls with their mother.

Meanwhile, since she has no daughter, she's placed more concern on her own social life.

"Kevin, would you come on, boy?" I pleaded. Kevin finally passed the game's controls to Kia.

"It's about time," I gasped.

"This was your idea."

"I know, Mom, but the game got heated."

Outside, I helped Kevin into the car and headed toward Broad Street. It would be a straight ride to the First Union Center from there.

Kevin was preoccupied with his Sixers' stat-sheet, but occasionally, he'd look up at me and smile. "Mom, can I ask you something without you trippin out on me?"

"I don't trip out."

"Yes. You do. Sometimes."

I braked at a red light and turned to Kevin. "Shoot."

"You ever plan on getting back with James?"

"That's simple. No."

"Any guy?"

"Why?"

"Never mind. See…you about ready to trip."

"Because I asked why?" I pulled away from the light at green.

The thought of James back in my life was unflattering. "You asked me a question, now I'm asking you one," I said.

Kevin palmed both ears. "Ah la…la…la…la…la…la," he sung, trying to drown out my question before it was asked. "Sike. What?" He asked. Still the child I love so much.

"Okay," I said as I turned onto Broad Street. "Are you worried about me being alone when you're away at college?"

"Not really…well, yeah. I don't know. I guess so."

"Well, don't. There's nothing at the moment that a man can do for me that I can't do for myself. Plus, I have enough to deal with at work and at home."

"But wouldn't it be nice to have a grown-up to talk to?"

"A grown-up?"

"Yeah."

I smiled at Kevin just enough to let him know that his message had seeped in. He was obviously tired of seeing me alone and under the impression that I need a man in my life to make me feel complete.

I hope I haven't raised a sexist, I thought, as I stopped at another red light.

We reached the First Union Center's parking lots after a two-block stall in traffic in route. I've been to three previous Sixers' games and wasn't surprised at all by the volume of cars, trucks, and pedestrians surrounding the arena. I managed to find a parking spot near the entrance. It was convenient to be able to park so close by, but also saddening to have to relive Kevin's misfortune each time I parked between two yellow strips of paint with the emblem of a wheelchair.

I helped Kevin from the car and rechecked each door. Kevin was already headed towards the entrance. I caught up. "You trying to leave me?" I asked.

"No." He looked up at me as I pushed the chair. Concern seemed to cover his narrow face and his eyes darted to the entrance then back to me.

My eyes followed his and then the blood raced to my head and I stopped in my tracks, wondered why the hell was Wesley here.

Kevin waved to Wesley. Then I knew. As much as I wanted to grip Kevin's throat and squeeze, I couldn't. I had to step back and recognize that Kevin has no idea of the complicated matchmaking he was trying to pull off. All the questions Kevin had asked during the ride suddenly made sense to me.

As we got closer to the building, I saw apprehension on Wesley's face, a nervousness in his stance.

He shook hands with Kevin then looked to me. "Why didn't you tell me that your mom was coming, too, Kevin?"

I guess it was Wesley's way of showing me that he hadn't staged our meeting.

"I wanted to surprise ya'll," Kevin grinned.

"You really should have checked with us first," said Wesley. I popped Kevin upside the head.

"Ow, Mom!"

"'Ow, Mom', nothing. You're dead wrong, boy."

Kevin rubbed the spot where I'd popped him. "I thought it would be good. Dang. Both of ya'll be acting like ya'll in love."

"Boy!" I snapped, wanted to place another pop upside his head, but he'd already wheeled himself out of distance, headed toward the entrance.

Wesley shrugged at the icy glare I shot his way and followed Kevin inside.

I hesitated, turned toward the parking area with ideas of leaving, but realized I couldn't. I felt trapped. No way could I leave Kevin with Wesley. I hurried through the entrance behind them, trying to compose myself.

The game was nearing half-time, with 2:08 to go in the second quarter, and the Sixers were down seven. They had been down twelve points only two minutes ago, but since their five to zero run, the twenty-three thousand fans were back to roaring and stomping.

Kevin and Wesley were among those with the loudest mouths. I felt completely out of the loop sitting so quietly. Every now and then, Kevin would turn to me and smile. I would return his smile and clap a little to disguise that my mind was mostly occupied with displeasure of having Wesley present. Although my initial anger had subsided a bit, I still wasn't able to enjoy the game. Too many memories clouded any enthusiasm I once had. It irked the hell out of me that Wesley could park his ass next to Kevin, a child he'd crippled during a shootout, accidentally or not, and cheer, high-five, and smile in Kevin's face as if he hadn't anything to do with Kevin's handicap.

A continuous chant of "DEFENSE! DEFENSE! DEFENSE..." sing-songed throughout the building each time the Knicks retained possession of the ball. And when Iverson stole the ball then stalled, at a dribble, at the top of the key with eighteen seconds left in the half, down just two, the entire arena was on their feet applauding the team's effort. Finally, Iverson shot the ball just before the buzzer sounded.

He missed.

"Awes" escaped the fans as they began reaching for jackets and personal items on their way to bathrooms and concession stands for half-time breaks. The three of us followed suit. I made sure it was me who wheeled Kevin out to the atrium.

"Let's get some pizza," Kevin stated, pointing to a standoff to the right.

We headed that way, ordered a whole cheese and mushroom pizza and large drinks before finding a table. I excused myself to use the restroom.

When I returned, Wesley was at the table, alone. I scanned the atrium for Kevin and couldn't spot him.

"Where's Kevin?" I asked him.

He sipped his drink and pointed toward an arcade. "I stayed so you'll know that we hadn't gone back to our seats."

"Don't do me any favors," I spat.

He nodded. "Still hate me, huh?"

"I don't hate anyone," I said pointedly. I breathed deeply to show my impatience. I even echoed my sentiment by eyeing my watch.

"I never had the chance to congratulate you for getting your degrees. Congratulations."

"Mm-hm," I hummed in acknowledgment. I hadn't sat down, just folded my arms across my chest, tapping my foot on the marble floor, and checked my watch again.

"I also think it's great that you've chosen child guidance as a career. You're good at it."

"And how would you know that…you being down Atlanta and all?"

"I saw it in you then, and in Kevin now. He…"

I raised a hand to cut his words short. "Please, Wesley. Can we just cut through the bullshit? We both know what you've done to my son's life — to my family's life. Now, tell me…what the hell do you want? Why can't you just leave us the hell alone? I did your ass a favor and not call the cops. Don't think I'll do it twice."

Wesley stared at the plastic cup in his hand and nodded. "You're right, Carol. You did me that favor and I'm grateful. But, even if I would have spent time in jail, I still would need and want to make things better for Kevin."

"By acting like you're his friend?"

"Not just a friend, but the kind of man he can look up to."

"Look up to?" My anger was rising. "You've killed somebody, Wesley. Whether it was a so-called accident or not, you've done something you can never undo or make up for." I pointed a stern finger at him. "I don't want my son around you, and I don't want you around my family either. The little financial package you left, consider it just-due." I spun and stormed off toward the arcade. My blood was boiling, and I could feel the tears welling in my eyes.

I had grown up surrounded by the exact lifestyle Wesley had been a part of, and I understood the circumstances that had, probably, led to the do-or-die situation that had gotten Kevin shot. But still, my heart wouldn't allow me to forgive Wesley for what he's done to my son. It would be sick to forgive him. Absolutely sick to allow him back into my life after everything I've found out about him. Sick.

But how could I explain the urges I get, the continuous desire to forgive him, to love him as I once had? My gut tells me that he regrets what he's done. His actions now show it and have always shown a desire for redemption. Still, the hurt he's caused seems unrepairable. To have to face him on a daily basis can only be sardonic.

Wesley sat quiet during most of the second half of the game. He was much more preoccupied with his thoughts, just as I had been during the first half. I sensed that Kevin recognized the barrier of tension between Wesley and I, especially when the game had ended, and Wesley and I parted ways in the parking area. What I had hoped to be a fun-filled evening with Kevin had turned out to be a sullen memory relived. That hurt and betrayal I had felt six years ago returned as if it had never gone.

On the drive home, I struggled to control the breaths that were gagging me like hiccups. But before I was able to gather myself, a tear streamed across my cheek. I saw that Kevin noticed.

"What's wrong?" Kevin asked.

I wiped away the tear. "Nothing's wrong."

"This is the second time you got all funny when Wes came around. What's going on between ya'll? Did he do something to you?"

"I said nothing's wrong, Kevin. Why can't you just leave it alone?"

Kevin turned to his window. "I'm not stupid, Mom. I know you used to see him before he left Philly."

I sniffled, placed an elbow on the door and rested my head in my palm. My eyes remained on the road, but I was remembering the cay I'd found the Armani shoebox filled with newspaper clippings of Kevin's accident and stacks of money in Wesley's closet, the day the truth had ripped my heart apart. But mostly, I was laboring over the secret I've been carrying with me for all of these years.

"Am I right?" Kevin asked.

"I don't want to talk about it, Kevin."

"Why? Do you still love him?"

I exhaled. "Please. Not now?"

Kevin and I rode the rest of the way home in silence. Usually, after a Sixers' win, Kevin was upbeat and talkative, but his obvious concern for me seemed to dampen his mood.

We entered the house to find Tonya at the table feasting on grilled cheese sandwiches.

Kevin headed straight to his bedroom.

I had sunk in a dining room chair next to Tonya, mentally exhausted.

"Damn, girl. You all right?" Tonya asked.

I picked up one of her two golden-brown sandwiches and tore away a piece. "You don't know the half of it."

"Can't be nothin' I ain't already heard before." Tonya bit into her sandwich.

"Mmmm. That's what you think."

"That bad, huh?"

"I don't even feel like talking about it. Are the girls in bed?"

"They fell out as soon as we got back. That damn Kelly is a trip. Her mouth is gettin' terrible."

"I told her about it."

"Well, you need to check her behind about it again. She cuss like a grown-ass man. I popped her once."

I nodded. My expression must have shown how I was feeling because Tonya pushed her plate away and glared at me.

"Tell me what happened," she insisted.

To my surprise, I did. I hesitantly started at the beginning and told her about the affair with Wesley, who he turned out to be, the money, and Wesley's transformation. Then I blurted it all out and still felt like I could've said more. When I was through talking, we both needed comforting.

Tonya was shaking her head, unbelievingly. "And you never told me til' now? All this time?"

"I know," I said defensively, "but I thought it was over. He left for Atlanta and…well, you know…"

Tonya snatched up her plate of, now, cold sandwiches and dumped them in the wastebasket. "You need to forget about this guy." She stared disgustingly.

"I don't believe you, Carol. All this time you knew who did that to Kevin."

I could only sit and absorb her outburst. I'd expected it. But, I had also expected her understanding. I was sure I'd get what I had hoped for after her initial shock. Minutes later, I did.

"I guess I'm the one to talk, huh?" She smiled wryly.

I gave a withdrawn grin at the memory of all the crazy, sexual 6-sci-pades Tonya had told me about. "I guess, some of you finally trickled in me," I replied.

She comforted me with a hug. "Everything's gonna be fine," she said.

I wondered if that were true.

CHAPTER 10

FELICIA

Three tiers of glass and brass store fronts, an escalator sit each end of the mall, air conditioning, and hordes of shoppers, with idle time to browse, make the Gallery an ideal place for bored teenagers to hangout and replenish from the outside heat. We'd been walking the Gallery for a little under an hour:

Cal, Mookie, Hasim, Celeste, Peaches, and I. Already, Hasim and Mookie had boosted two bags full of Kani jeans and belts, and we all had just finished profiling while trying on and assortment of designer sunglasses. We weren't able to boost any of those, so, Celeste wanted to buy a pair; however, the store's manager had asked us to leave on account of all the commotion we had caused. Peaches had called the white, dainty woman every cuss name in the book before we left, and now, as we sat lounging on and around a stone bench, Celeste and Peaches were criticizing the females strolling by, styling in the latest fashions.

"Oooooh, she know she wrong with all that weave," Celeste declared, high-fiving Peaches.

"Don't front like you ain't never have no weave," Mookie interjected.

"Not all the way to my ass," Celeste responded.

"Stop lying, girl. We all know that somebody's weave's been near your ass."

We all broke out in laughter. All but Celeste. She rolled her eyes instead.

Although Celeste is gay, she carries herself in a feminine way, not all Butch which is cool.

For half an hour more we sat and watched shoppers amble by. Many sauntered by, gawking at the mall's elaborate interior.

The soft music from the mall's speakers began to bore me to death. We were all becoming a bit restless just sitting around and welcomed Hasim's suggestion to head to the mall's arcade.

On the way, we visited Rattles & Bibs, and everyone told Hasim and me what would look good on our baby. Five minutes after leaving the store, Celeste and Peaches handed me six boosted baby outfits and begged me to let the two of them share the god mom responsibilities.

Hasim, Cal, and Mookie talked while we walked, already introducing my unborn child to the thug-life. I listened to the three of them talk.

"Shorty gonna be cold, Yo," Cal was saying. "I can see 'I'm now, shufflin' ho's like' a decka cards."

"Nigga, please," said Hasim. "My little homie gonna be strictly 'bout a dollar. I'ma train Lil 'sim to recognize busters on sight and to hold down his own. Niggas gonna know if they come up against him, shit ain't gonna be sweet."

"True that" Cal responded, nodding.

"I guess I gotta be the one to school Lil 'Sim bout hoops and shit, huh?" Mookie asked. "'Cause you niggas ain't got no games."

"Fool, you trippin," Hasim gushed. "I crushed you!"

Soon the guys' attentions were on sports.

I tsked loud enough to let Hasim know that I wasn't getting enough of his attention.

"Yo, I'm outta that. My boo gettin' all soft on me," he announced, ending his conversation, and wrapping a tattooed arm around my waist.

On the way down, Hasim whispered to me, "Why you trippin, bay?" He placed a palm on my belly and kissed my neck. My spot.

I melted against him and wished we were alone. Hasim's always more affectionate when his crew's not around. He didn't want to appear soft in front of them. Sometimes I mind being second to Hasim's image, then I remind myself of how important images are in the ghetto. I knew who and what Hasim was when we hooked up and didn't want to become one of those females who tries to change their man, after the fact. Hasim is who he is.

The small arcade was nearly empty of people. Cal and Mookie peeled away to a shooting booth, Hasim leaped into the seat of a car-like game, and Celeste and Peaches took off to a photo booth, leaving me standing alone. Fine friends they are, I thought.

Drowned in ringing bells, varooms, and screeches, and arcade gunfire, I pushed two quarters into a Matrix pinball machine and fought to keep each ball in play more than twenty seconds. I've never been good at pinball. Two dollars later, I was behind the car game that Hasim was fixated with, watching him race toward a high score.

"I'ma show you how it's done, bay," boasted Hasim.

I smiled down at him as his body twitched and swayed with the car's movements speeding on the screen. He'd stomp on the brake and holler "Oh shit!" every now and then. It was obvious Hasim thought of himself as a world class driver.

We left the arcade after an hour, rowdy as ever. Again, Peaches took up talking about passersby. This time, Cal and Mookie joined her.

"Ya'll, need to cut it out," I said, stopping to admire a leather jacket I had noticed earlier. "Oooh, baby, get me this?" I asked Hasim.

"You already got a leather."

"Not like this one."

"Yo, dawg, that shit's phat," Cal chimed.

"I'm goin' in," said Mookie. "I know they got some wicked gear."

"Niggah, you ain't buyin' nuttin'" Cal said.

"That don't mean a playa cornin' out empty handed."

The inside of the store was larger than I thought. Two salespersons were behind a large counter when we entered. One came around to wait on us. A young, black female wearing silver necklaces and blue tinted glasses.

"Can I help you all?" she asked, her voice an even soprano.

"Nah. We cool right now," Mookie answered.

"All of you?"

"Ain't that what I said?"

We scattered throughout the store. Out of the corner of my eye, I watched the suspicion rise on the girl's face as she casually followed Mookie and Cal.

Celeste and Peaches were headed toward the rear of the store while Hasim and I checked out the leather jackets displayed at the store's front. They were identical to the black jacket I had noticed in the store window only of a variety of blues, reds, greens, and beiges.

"This bad boy got my name all over it," I squealed, trying on a blood-red jacket.

"Get it then," Hasim encouraged.

"I don't have the money."

"Who said anything 'bout buyin' it?" Hasim's expression was one of seriousness. "If you want it, I'll spin the chick at the desk." Without waiting for me to answer, Hasim set the bag he was carrying next to me and walked to the counter.

My eyes darted around the store for my friends, but mostly for the young black girl. She was caught up in Cal and Mookie's bullshit. The time seemed ripe.

"Fuck it," I mumbled, snatching the jacket from the rack. I stuffed it into the bag then looked back at Hasim. He'd spun the female at the desk 180 degrees. My heart was pounding away, and my hands were moist as baby wipes. Back and forth my eyes darted. I picked up the bag. "Come on, bay," I called to Hasim, "I gotta pee."

Hasim pointed to the door. "Then go 'head. We'll catch up."

That was my cue to leave. With each step toward the store's glass doors, I bitched and moaned as if I were upset that Hasim would not leave with me. My heart could beat no faster.

When the alarm began beeping as I passed through the doorway, all eyes turned toward me then to the bag that I was carrying.

I hadn't seen any alarms on the jacket and stared down at the bag, dumbfounded.

"Excuse me, miss," the cashier called after me. "Can you walk back through?"

My nervousness quickly turned into survival mode and my guard raised. "Walk back through where?" I questioned.

"Through the doorway."

"She ain't gotta walk back through nothin'!" Hasim barked. "Go 'head to the bathroom, bay."

"The alarm went off, sir. Yes. She does."

By now, Celeste and Peaches were pushing me through the door. More beeps sounded.

"Excuse me!" the cashier shouted. She was already on the phone.

I quick stepped toward the escalator with my girls on my heels.

Hasim, Cal, and Mookie lingered behind, still arguing with the black girl who was screaming for me to stop.

"Hurry up, girl!" Peaches ordered. Sha was pulling wool sweaters from around her waist and stuffing them into the bag. We had only reached the escalator and already I was huffing and puffing. I tried not to look back but couldn't help myself.

Behind me, I saw the guys sprint onto the escalator. When I reached the bottom, a huge hand gripped my wrist. My eyes bounced from the hand then to my right where two white security guards were grabbing Celeste and Peaches. I tried to snatch away, but the vise grip had a firm hold of me.

"I need you to come with us," the guard grabbing me stated.

He was a bear of a man with too much hair on his face. "For what?!" I cried.

"You'll find out. Just come with us."

Celeste and Peaches had given up without a fight.

I wasn't about to. "I'm not goin' a damn place!" I yelled then began thrashing about wildly, still clutching the bag of stolen merchandise. Sweaters flew from the bag as I tussled with the bear-like man. After more fruitless struggling, I tried out and was handcuffed, lifted off of my feet and ushered through the mall.

I noticed Hasim, Cal, and Mookie looking on with blank expressions. I just kept yelling, "I'M PREGNANT! I'M PREGNANT! DON'T HURT MY BABY!!!" Hands were beneath my armpits, lifting and sliding my feet across the marble floor. "GET OFF ME! GET OFFA ME!!!!" I felt the bag's handle being pried from my fingers. Then it was gone. My head spun in the direction where I had seen Hasim. He was gone, too. In front of me were my girls, handcuffed and walking, cussing up a storm. Shoppers were watching us with open stares. I wondered if the people who Celeste and Peaches had made fun of were returning the favor. I knew I was making a spectacle of myself. But I didn't care.

Three hours had to have passed when I decided to stop pacing and sit still in the tiny, dank cell I had been taken to.

Everything was of concrete, steel or metal which gave the hole a biting chill. The air conditioning, sweeping through the three-cell area didn't help matters much, and my only view was of a bare wall beyond the steel bars.

I shivered and wondered if the cold was a ploy to discourage busted shoplifters not to visit the store again. How could I have been so stupid? I asked myself. I hadn't bothered to check the pockets of the leather jacket. That's where tiny packet alarms were. I kicked the porcelain toilet. "Shit!"

At the sound of jingling keys, I gripped the steel bars. "Hey!" I yelled.

The jingling faded. I had been ignored.

I breathed deeply then plopped onto the metal bunk with no mattress, wished I hadn't because a sharp pain shot from my rear up to my belly. Tears had begun forming. The last thing I wanted or needed was to birth my child in prison — over a leather jacket. I once heard that when you give birth to a child in prison, the child becomes a product of The System as well; especially in my case, where there's no one who'll be willing to take the responsibility of raising the baby while I'm away.

Again, I heard keys jingling. This time, I fought the urge to run to the bars.

The outer door opened and the huge security guard, who'd handcuffed me, appeared at the cell. Earlier, I heard one of the security guards refer to him as Jay.

I stared back. Played tough. "Ya'll, gonna let me call my mother of what?" I barked. "I'm a juvenile and I'm pregnant. I know this is illegal."

He grinned. "In a minute. Simmer down. And no. This isn't illegal."

"Well, I ain't got a minute."

"Sure, you do."

A white, older man entered the holding area and stood next to Jay.

"What do you think?" Jay asked him.

"About what?"

"About giving Knight here a call."

"How long's it been?"

"Three hours," I snapped.

The second man shrugged slim shoulders. "I don't care. Write her up a summons while you're at it. If nobody picks her up, send her to juvey."

It was obvious neither man wanted to deal with the likes of me, so I sat there pouting, contemplating whether getting a message to my mother was insane. In Mama's eyes, I'm already a worthless slut who'll never amount to anything, and knowing her, she'd probably leave me stewing til' the baby's due. No way would she allow me to live down getting arrested — even after the baby is born. Uh-uh. Mama's voice wasn't one I'd like to hear.

At the thought of juvenile detention, goosebumps ran the length of my body. For the third time, since being locked in this cold, brutal cage, I pulled the piece of paper, with the scribbled numbers, from my pants pocket and stared at it. I closed my eyes and palmed it.

It was my last hope.

CHAPTER 11

WESLEY

The wedding had taken place before Sheila's church congregation, The Mount Zion Baptist Memorial, in the heart of North Philadelphia. More than one hundred guests had arrived for the ceremony. Sheila's homegirl and confidant, Patricia, had filled the roll of Maid of Honor, and several of Sheila's nieces acted as bridesmaids. Two of Patricia's daughters, five and seven, drowned in white to match the arrangement of flowers, performed the duties of flower girls.

Throughout the ceremony, Stacks had been nervous. All his sluggishness had been erased and draped in the well-tailored tux; he had never looked more ready to flee from embarrassment. Little Bro had been that nervous. My only wish had been to have had Benny witness him. We could've dragged this one out for years.

The wedding reception was different. It was slightly smaller with a majority of family and friends in attendance.

Sheila had rented the first floor of a banquet hall that had been decorated with religious tapestries and pink paper buntings stretching clear across a high, eggshell ceiling. Plates, bowls and huge trays of soul food had been catered in and lie invitingly atop of laced, linen-clothed tables at the room's rear. The rest of the space was being used for festivities, and many of the seats, surrounding circular tables, stayed empty of bodies because the party was definitely on the dancefloor. We had already gotten through the bride and groom's ceremonious lead dance. And now, Sheila and Stacks were leading the ghetto rendition of the Electric Slide.

I had cut away from the dancing and laughter just before the dance ended and the next song began, was parlaying beside the rose-sculptured soda fountain when Missy grabbed my attention. She was backing away from the buffet, plate in hand.

"Hey you," I greeted.

She turned to me, surprised. "Hey yourself, stranger."

"I thought that was you backing that thing up."

She blushed, sat her plate down and hugged me.

Missy and I had had a thing back in high school. Although our making out had never reached third base, they had easily rounded second.

"How you been?" she asked.

"Busy."

"Atlanta, right?"

I raised an eyebrow and she smiled.

"I've been keeping up on you," she admitted.

"Why's that?"

"Oh, just because."

"Don't tell me you've matured into a stalker."

Her high-pitched laugh turned a few heads. "No, silly. I asked your brother how you were. That's how I knew about the wedding."

Musiq's "Don't Change" echoed from the wall-mounted speakers. "Oooooh. That's my jam," Missy cooed. "Come on and dance with me." She grabbed my wrist.

"Nah. I don't think so."

"Uh-uh. You gonna dance with me." Her tone was definite, and before I could refuse again, my feet were two-stepping to Musiq's harmony.

Dancing with Missy stirred many memories. She was still as phine as I remember and plenty of male eyes were swooping in on her voluptuous booty that seemed to be sweltering in *a* tight, lime ankle-length dress. Her skin was an unblemished, deep chocolate that could easily give most men an instant sweet tooth. The feel of Missy's body pressing against mine, combined with her flowery scent, sent my mind swirling back to when we were teens. I shuddered at the memory of how wet she used to get when we made out and eased my pelvis back to avoid her peeping my excitement. It was too late.

"You remember, huh?" she whispered while cupping the back of my neck with one hand and caressing my back with the other.

"Of course, I remember. It's kinda hard to forget."

"I know. We were something back then."

"Yes. We were," I agreed, regretting never having gone all the way.

The song ended and reluctantly we separated. Our eyes met, and I could tell that she was remembering, too.

"You still with Keith?" I asked.

She nodded and sighed what seemed to be regret. "We have two boys now. Keith's been doing odd jobs here and there, but we're surviving."

"That's good to know. But how about you?"

"How about me what?"

"You happy? Working?"

"I'm content. I work part-time doing clerical work for a real estate company downtown. It's not that bad."

"At least you're happy. That's what counts."

It was obvious from Missy's demeanor that she and Keith are having problems. I almost felt a bit of pity for her — until I remembered her cheating and giving her virginity to Keith and not me. The hard-on I had had for her evaporated. "Listen. I have some best man business to take care of right now. How about I hold you to a second dance when I'm through?"

She smiled. "Sure. I'll be here."

I walked away wondering if she was recalling her deceit and disloyalty. Seeing her gave me a dose of my past that I could do without. Missy had provided my first taste of life's heartbreaks. And women say it's always the men.

I strolled to the bar then to the small stage where the dee-jay had a mic set up. I clicked it on, blew into the mic twice while tapping it the same many times. "Testing…testing. Can I have your attentions, please?"

When the dee-jay stopped the music, the dancing and chatter ceased also. All eyes were on me. "As the wedding's best man, we all know that I'm required to say a little somethin-somethin to toast this blessed union we all have the pleasure of partaking upon."

Stacks and Sheila were seated at a front table, holding hands, and smiling. I continued. "I'm just as surprised as all of you at how my baby brother managed to find such a warm and wonderful woman to put up with him." A buzz of laughter rose. "I just wish someone hypnotize Mary-J for me." More laughter.

"On a serious note, though. There are some couples who are ideal for one another and Sheila and Stacks are one of those such couples. I'm certain that they're love and respect for one another will last forever. To the bride and groom. Much Love."

We all raised our glasses in toast of the newlyweds, who played their parts by sharing a warm kiss. I was genuinely glad for the two of them after having watched them struggle through rough times. And just knowing that Stacks is making a serious effort to slow down is gratifying.

An hour passed before Stacks was pulling me from the dancefloor and out of Missy's grasp. "I'm 'bout ready to fade," he said. He was sporting a wide grin, slanted eyes and had full bottle of Courvoisier gripped at its neck.

"I see you getting your buzz on. You gonna make it to your honeymoon all right?"

"I'm straight, dawg. We doin' the designated driver thing. How 'bout you? Missy been clockin you like mad, yo."

"She tryna make up for crossing a brotha back in the day."

Stacks poked my chest with a forefinger. "That's why you gotta settle down, dawg."

"Look who's talking."

He flashed his ringed finger at me. "Hey, I can talk."

All I could do is smile. "Okay. You frontin, right?"

"Damn Skippy."

I gave him a dap. "So, what now? You outie for a few?"

"Coupla weeks. I'ma holla, though."

I gave Stacks a hug and congratulated him again. Sheila came and stood beside him, grabbed her husband's arm. "Thank you, Wesley," she said.

"You're welcome, sis. If he start acting up, don't hesitate to call."

She eyed Stacks, lovingly. "I won't."

After giving Sheila a hug and kiss, I was watching the two of them walk away when Missy arrived and handed me a Heineken. She was wearing a smile that reminded me of the problems that Pam and I were having in our relationship. I hadn't thought about Pam much during my trip and was surprised she hadn't phoned me much.

It hadn't taken Missy much to persuade me to take her back to my hotel room so that we could finish catching up on old times. She had already made herself comfortable on the hotel sofa, curled dancer's calves beneath her and was tracing tiny circles on one chocolate thigh. Nervousness kept me behind the tiny bar longer than usual.

"Whatever happened to poor old Lenny Booth?" I asked, dropping two ice cubes into a rum and Coke.

"Three finger Lenny? He met some big ol' country girl and went south somewhere."

"Get outta here."

"Smiley, too."

"Crooked teeth Smiley?"

"Mm-hm. Hardly nobody from back then live around the neighborhood anymore. Everybody picking up and moving. Especially since they tore down the projects."

"I heard." I carried our drinks to the sofa and handed Missy her scotch before parking beside her.

She gulped more than half of the scotch and set down the glass. "Do you plan on moving back to Philly?" she asked. Her coal-black pupils showed interest or hope. It was hard to tell which.

"Been thinking about it for a while, but so much of my life is in Atlanta now."

"That's too bad," she purred then slid closer to me.

I stood and grabbed her near-empty glass just as she began leaning in for a kiss. "Would you like a refill?" I offered.

She giggled. "Sure. Why not?"

At the mini-bar I downed my own drink. The effects from the earlier alcohol had begun taking their toll. I reached for the bottle of scotch, turned, and Missy was there.

"Wesley, I get the feeling that you're trying to push me away."

"Push you away? Why would you say that?"

"A girl knows."

"Really?"

"Yes. Really."

She'd cornered me and pressed her body against mine while she toyed with my dreds. I tried masking my arousal and continued pouring her drink, overpoured it and reached for a napkin.

She grabbed my hand. "What's the matter, baby? Aren't you a bit curious about what we missed out on?" She pressed herself even harder against me.

"That was a long time ago, Missy."

"Yeah…And…?"

"And things are different now."

"And…?" Her hands were wandering, found their way across the zipper of my pants. She squeezed.

"And we both have relationships."

My zipper came down and Missy's hand was inside my slacks, probing then groping.

"I won't tell if you won't," she tempted.

My mind tried to resist, but my body was responding to Missy's touch, her seduction. For years after she had dumped me, I had wondered just what it would've been like to lose myself within her depth. And now, there was nothing between us but air and opportunity. Hungrily, I kissed her, tasted the scotch lingering on her active tongue. Her kisses ventured the length of my torso and, in one motion, she was taking me into her mouth. I closed my eyes and moaned. My head fell back. "Ahhhhh. Shhhiiiit. Missy, we can't do this. Mmmmmm…no. Ohhhhh."

She didn't speak or try to stop. I felt her humming "Mmmmms" and tried prying her head away. She kept at it, fighting my will to lift her from me.

"Come on now. Stop," I managed. This time I pushed her head as hard as I could and plopped from her mouth.

She stood. "Stop trippin and enjoy this. Nobody will ever know."

I hurried to tuck myself away. "But I'll know."

"Oh God!" she shrieked. "Don't tell me you've found some morality." She stomped from the bar and began pulling on her shoes. "This whole thing has, obviously, been a big mistake."

I stared at her magnificent ass bouncing away and couldn't believe that I was turning down the opportunities it presented, to finally make good on one of my childhood regrets. "Missy, wait. Let me explain."

She held up a palm and continued snatching up her things. "You don't have to explain. I understand."

"No. You don't."

She paused to stare daggers at me. It was obvious that a woman as phine as Missy didn't take kindly to rejection. But what did she expect after dumping me?

"It's not you, Missy. It's me. I'm going through some things with the relationship I'm already in. I don't need any more complications right now."

"Complications? What's complicated about sex, Wesley? Wham bam and it's over." She tsked. "You know what…? I'm outta here. It's all good."

I grabbed Missy's wrist. "Don't be like this. We can still chill and have a good time."

She snatched away, visibly upset. "It's fine, Wesley." At the door, she spun to face me. "Thanks for reminding me of why I dumped your ass!" She slammed shut the door. The vibrations knocked over a vase on the foyer table.

I breathed deeply and stared at the closed door. I needed a cold shower. On my way, I wondered if I'll ever understand the mind of a woman.

CHAPTER 12

CAROL

Sometimes taking a chance on someone can inspire them or spark some hope within that person. I can easily remember the times in my life when I, myself, had not receiving encouragement and guidance, had been turned away by foster parents whose concerns revolved around my well-being. Back then, it had seemed so difficult believing in myself, so abnormal for my life to somehow reach normality. I had often found myself surviving within a state of depression while smiling on the outside. It had been so important for me, back then, to know that there was someone who cared, really cared, and had not look down on me because of the faults that I had made. I had promised myself then that I'd never be that kind of person, that kind of parent to my children. Perhaps that's why when I received Felicia's phone call for help, I decided to take a chance on her. Lord knows she needs someone to help steer her away from the thugs and vagabonds she runs with.

Now, as I sit and wait for Felicia to be released into my custody, I thought about what the store's detectives had told me about her shoplifting. I was trying to suppress my anger at the stupidity of her actions after a half hour of waiting when Felicia, belly, and all, emerged from a back room looking haggard and frowning. I tried imaging just what she had gone through then decided that whatever it had been, I hope it had been worth the chance she had taken. I rose from the straight back, without a word to her and signed a guardian responsibility form that comforted the store's detectives that Felicia would attend a shoplifters' anonymous session two weeks from today.

When we stepped from the store and were walking through the Gallery is when Felicia finally spoke.

"I'm sorry I had to call you," she muttered.

I asked what I had thought about the entire drive downtown. "Why not call your mother?"

She rubbed her belly and shrugged, displayed her adolescence.

It was disappointing.

"What's wrong with you, Felicia?"

She twisted her lips and eyed the ceiling. "Ain't nothin' wrong with me. I got caught that's all."

"Got caught?"

"Yeah."

"And everybody supposed to suffer because of your selfishness, huh?"

She finally squared her eyes with mine. "Can we get outta here now?" she asked.

"Yeah. We can go…for now. Just know that we have some talking to do."

She tsked as we headed out of the Gallery.

An evening's darkness had fallen on Philadelphia and the heavy, downtown traffic rolled by us as we stood at the curb.

"Are you hungry?" I asked.

"A little."

"Well, I'm starved." I dug into my jean's pocket to be certain I had brought along enough cash. I had. "Come on, let's get something to eat. I know you're not in a hurry."

We wound up at a small diner on one of center city's tiny, back streets behind Chestnut. I'd passed the diner several times before but had never venture inside.

Two uniformed waitresses smiled a lot in the dim interior and alternated between six square tables lined against the walls. Although the kitchen was hidden behind two thick, oak doors, the aroma, seeping from beneath the cracks, would entice recognition that a lot of love was being put into the preparation of their meal.

Felicia and I were seated near the rear of the half-filled restaurant. Felicia was wearing a funky expression to match her stank attitude, and I was feeling some hesitancy considering I'd taken a huge risk and much interest in her well-being. One thing I was certain of: I wasn't about to allow her to spoil my appetite. My stomach was growling.

As soon as the waitress placed the straw basket of freshly-baked bread on our table, I went to work on it, tore then buttered a chunk of bread while scanning the menu. I looked over my menu at Felicia just sitting there quiet and withdrawn. "Are you going to feed that child?" I asked.

She tsked then picked up her menu which caused me to drop mine to the table.

"I hope this isn't your way of showing me gratitude for coming all the way down here to help you?"

"No," she simply said, "it's not you. I'm mad at Hasim."

I picked up my menu. "Oh, him."

"Why you say it like that?"

"Like what?"

"You know…'oh, him'. Like he don't matter?"

"Did I? I guess I think as much of him as you do right now."

"You don't even know him."

"Sure, I do. I hope you don't think that how he treats you is that unique? But that's your business." I pretended my focus was on the menu, but actually, I was hoping she'd take the bait and open up. So far, she only sat stewing.

The waitress, a thin, white woman around twenty with bunned, auburn hair, interrupted. "Have you ladies decided on anything yet?"

I quickly made my selection and ordered the country-fried steak, fries, and iced tea. Felicia ordered fried turkey-sausage, baked potato, and pineapple soda.

When the waitress had gone and I'd buttered a second hunk of bread, Felicia spoke. "Hasim's not a bad person."

"No? Tell me what kind of person you consider bad."

"A murderer. Rapist. People like that. Hasim might get in fights and stuff, but that stuff's petty compared to some 'the things people be doin'."

I finished chewing. "Listen, Felicia, I'm not concerned about Hasim as much as I'm concerned about you. Hasim is grown."

"I'm fine."

"Ha!" I blurted. "You out here boosting and getting locked up, and you sitting here saying you're fine? I don't think so, sweetheart. Your problems are just beginning."

Felicia took her slow time about buttering a chunk of the bread. I sensed her insecurities and felt that she was experience the doubt carried by many young, expecting mothers. I recalled when I was pregnant at her age and a pang of concern shot through me. The fear and lack of confidence that I had felt back then had taken a long time to pass. There hadn't been a lot of positives for me to have had considered.

From what I already know about Felicia, she'll have a long, tough days and nights ahead of her.

Our food arrived and immediately sent my stomach on a loop.

I doused ketchup on my fries and dug in, forgot all about the few patrons around us, licked my fingers and all. It surprised me to see that Felicia was doing no better. I guessed that after spending hours behind bars, her appreciation of a good meal had tripled. Half through us wolfing down our meals, the conversation picked back up.

"Are you gonna tell my mom I got locked up?" Felicia asked.

"I'm not sure. Ethically, I wasn't supposed to come get you. We both were wrong."

"So, you not gonna say nothin?"

"I guess it really depends."

"I've never been locked up before."

I bit a fry. "I know. But the first time is a start."

"I don't even know why I did it. I guess, I feel like I'm losing Hasim and wanted to show him that I'm still down for him."

I closed my eyes and shook my head. "I don't want to judge either of you, however, that was a stupid thing to do. And for a ridiculous reason at that."

"I know that now."

"I sure hope so because I can't be the one to bail you out of this kind of trouble again. I could lose my job over this." I reached across the table and grabbed hold of her hand. "Sweetheart, you are about to experience one of God's greatest miracles. Don't let your insecurities over some guy influence your decisions that could affect the rest of your life." I paused. "I want to try and help you through this, Felicia, but you have to promise me that you'll make better decisions concerning this baby."

"I know, I know."

"Yeah, well, that's easy to say. Doing it is an entirely different thing."

The waitress arrived with the check. "Is that it?"

I grabbed the check. "For me it is. You all done?" I asked Felicia. She nodded.

I felt somewhat better about where she was headed, patted her hand, and hoped to God that she takes my advice.

During the drive to North Philly, we made small talk about child-care. We had just turned off of Broad Street and onto Girard Avenue when we noticed the firetrucks double-parked at the project's lip. A flurry of activity surrounded the trucks. I slowed the car to scan the commotion.

"What's goin' on?" Felicia asked.

"I don't know. Something's on fire."

A police officer was standing in the middle of the street directing traffic to turn left, away from the scene. Before I turned left, I was able to witness a crowd of onlookers, a police barricade, and more firetrucks. Firemen were scurrying around a housing project's burning two-story apartment. "Something's definitely burning," I said aloud.

Felicia was in her seat, on edge. It startled me when she began yelling, "Oh, my God! Oh, my God!" Fear seemed to have gripped her. "Stop the car! Stop!" she screamed.

I pulled the car to the curb and Felicia scrambled out of the passenger-side door. "Connie! Oh, my God, Connie! My sister!"

It dawned on me that the burning two-story was where Felicia lived. I stumbled out of the car behind her. "Felicia, wait!" Before I could catch up to her, the traffic cop had grabbed hold of her arm and was struggling to keep his grip. I caught up to them and tried holding on to her for dear life. Trying to grab hold of Felicia was like gripping a handful of the wind. Her struggling eased, however, her sobs were heartbreaking. "Where is she?" she groaned. "Connie, please, don't be there!"

A fire-fighter emerged from the building carrying an unconscious child. Felicia lunged out of our grasp, and before we could react, she had broken through our waving arms. We both gave chase. She didn't stop until she'd reached the crowd, who stood yelling and pointing. On the sidewalk is where paramedics stooped attending to Connie. Felicia stood over them in a state of hysteria. I held her around the waist and watched the paramedics administer CPR to a still unconscious Connie.

"Please, help her. Please, help her…" Felicia was mumbling. I hugged her even tighter and prayed.

Minutes passed and still Connie lay unconscious. "Get her in the vehicle," one medic ordered. "She's still not responding."

Suddenly Felicia's weight crashed onto me. Her sobs became groans and she collapsed.

"Somebody help me!" I screamed while struggling to hold her up.

Two fire-fighters hurried over.

"It's her house," I told one. "She's pregnant."

Felicia let loose an eerie cry and groped at her belly. "Nooooo!" she moaned as we edged her toward an ambulance.

My head was swooning, and my temples were thumping. I raced to my car, grabbed the steering wheel with shaky hands and wiped the tears from my eyes. I fumbled with my purse and pulled out my cellphone. It would be a long night. I needed to call home.

CHAPTER 13

WESLEY

I've only been gone for a few days, but the way Pam has been clinging to me, you would think that it's been years since we've saw one another or made love. Sex has always been an adventure between us. I'd thought we'd turned every corner possible and knew for certain that we've experimented with every position the Karma Sutra has to offer. But truth be told, Pam's mind is one for the wicked.

I'd made it home — back in Atlanta -- during the wee hours.

As much as I loved being in Philly, my temptations had weighed heavy. During my flight back, I found myself rehearsing my answers to questions that I was sure Pam would ask about the wedding and especially the bachelor party. And as much as I wanted to forget my experience with Missy, her seduction had created a sexual frustration in me that was the cause of me running home for some loving — and loving is just what Pam had given. All the way through morning rush hour and then some.

I had dosed off to sleep, opened my eyes and felt as drained as if I'd completed a twelve-round fight with Lennox Lewis.

Pam and I were tangled in one another's arms, naked atop of Gucci bedspreads. She was staring at me, and I sensed where our conversation would soon be heading, so I saved her the trouble of asking and began summarizing my trip, left out the parts about Carol and Missy. Each time I tried to conversate about the wedding ceremony, she'd interrupt me with questions about the bachelor party and because she knows Stacks, she questioned me about the get high.

"Stacks and a couple of fellas had a little weed, but no, nobody did any of the hard stuff," I answered.

"Mm-hm. I can only imagine."

I twisted my arms from around her. "Pam, why do you always expect the worst from everybody?"

"I don't."

"Yes. You do."

"Maybe it's because it's hard to expect much from the thugs that your brother hangs out with."

"You haven't seen Stacks in years, let alone any of the people he be with."

Pam wrapped my arms back around her and snuggled against me. "If you see one dope dealer, you've seen 'em all."

I used to deal, I thought. I choked back the cussing out I wanted to give her but didn't want to say something I might later regret.

Pam is so high-strung on herself. During our college days at Temple University, she'd been much the same way. Back then, all she had to boast about were her parents' money and a huge trust fund. Now that her fashion career has taken off and she's accumulated her own wealth, her bourgeois attitude has worsened. Her button nose is always pointing upward, and more and more her attitude has been testing my nerves.

Again, I tried to change the subject. This time I chose a subject she adores talking about. Herself.

"How'd the fashion show go?" I asked.

Excitement sprung to Pam's face. "Oh, it was soooo perfect.

You should've seen how buyers were gawking at the new designs and scribbling names on checks. I couldn't've asked for a better premier for the winter lines."

I was untangling myself from her when she stopped me. "Don't get up. I want to talk to you about something."

"About what?"

"Come on. Lay back down."

Skeptically, I did as she asked. She welcomed me with warm, soft nakedness. My nostrils filled with her vanilla fragrance as I settled back into her arms.

"You know I'm not getting any younger, right?" she asked getting comfortable.

I wasn't about to answer that one, so, I laid quiet.

"You listening?"

"Yeah, I'm listening. You're twenty-eight."

"Twenty-seven," she corrected, lightly tapping my cheek.

"My bad."

"Hush, Wesley. I'm trying to ask you something."

"Go ahead."

"Thank you." She paused. "Okay. Here it is…I'm ready to have kids," she blurted.

Oooooh! my mind hollered. It felt as if my thoughts had been sucker-punched. My body tensed and I was lost for words.

"Well?" she prodded. "Well, what?"

She hadn't been looking at me throughout her spiel but now she was. Her eyes were questioning, filled with hope and possibility.

"Whoa!" I mustered.

"Whoa? Is that all you can say?"

Right away I knew that I had reacted wrong. I did the manly thing and humbly laughed it off. "Where is all of this coming from?" I asked.

"Uh-uh." She sat up, out of my reach, and stared at me. "Seriously, Pam. You never mentioned kids before. I never pictured you as the mother type."

"Mm-hm." Her eyes became thin slits.

I saw the anger brewing on her face, rolled out of bed, found my drawers, and went and sat at my computer. Out of the corner of my eye, I saw Pam slip into a pair of sweats. She'd come to stand over me, staring at what it felt to be through my dreds, my scalp and skull, all to get a peek at what I was thinking. Her silence was typical of her anger. I expected an explosion.

"And why don't you see me as the mother type?"

I pushed the computer's mouse aside and faced her. "Pam, all you've ever thought about is what's best for you and your career. You don't cook, wash clothes, do dishes, none of the domestic stuff that one would expect a mother to do. That's why."

"So?"

"So? You telling me that you're ready to have children and make somebody besides yourself a priority?" I laughed. "I can see you hiring a nanny already."

Her gaze drifted away from me. I knew that I'd struck a nerve because her arms folded across her body and she began tapping a bare foot on the carpet.

It wasn't as if I didn't want children in my life. Having children is something I've thought about for years. It's just that I'm not ready to marry Pam, and Pam certainly isn't ready for marriage to me. We've had the discussion about marriage only months ago when we had found out about Stacks' wedding.

"I guess, I'll just have to learn how to do some of those things," Pam said.

I stood and turned Pam's disappointed face toward me. "Sweetheart, we have plenty of time to make babies, okay? Just because things are kind of rough between us now, let's not make believe that kids will make things better." I pecked Pam's lips.

"I'm losing you, Wesley. I can tell."

I pulled her into me. "You're not losing me, baby. I'm right here." My chest had smothered her words, but it sounded like she had said "For how long?" I led Pam back to the bed and laid with her. I, too, wondered if I were slowly drifting away from what Pam and I share. I wondered how long it would take, laid still, and struggled with the question until I could lie still no longer. When she'd drifted asleep, I got up and tiptoed to the computer.

Although I wasn't required to venture into work until the next day, I dragged through my office door a little after 11am. A pile of memos had been left for me to review along with a stack of paperwork to deal with, work that I believed I would be ready to tackle. I settled behind my desk and realized that it wasn't the job I was rushing to, but away from Pam's whining.

I'd just begun laboring through the pile of papers when Julius burst in the office. He was all excited and hurriedly took a seat across from me.

"How was it," he gushed.

I tossed my pen on the desk and sat back. "Typical wedding. Flowers, cake, dancing, you know."

"Not that. The bachelor party. You put your thing down, right, dawg?"

I smiled. "And you know this."

"Strippers?"

"Yep."

"Seven? Eight?"

"About that."

"Oh, shit! Sukie-sukie." Julius' eyes were dancing. Although he dresses the part of a suave and debonair businessman, he was quite opposite in character. "I bet the brothas were hittin' skins all night," he stated.

"Nah, man, it was all fun with the girls."

"Huh?" Julius' expression held skepticism. "Aw, Wes, don't tell me the train ain't run through Philly."

"Sorry, bro."

He sat back in the chair, and I picked back up my pen. "What a waste," he remarked. "The one chance you get to cut up without the ball and chain and you don't even take it. I would've been spanking ass all night long."

Again, I tossed my pen down. This time in frustration. "What's up, Julius? I got a pile of work I gotta catch up on.

He stood. "Damn. You can't holla at your dawg?"

"Nah, it's not that. My bad. I'm flexed about something else."

"Something else?"

I nodded the kind of nod that said shit is deep.

He pointed. "I told you, didn't I?"

"Told me what, Julius?"

"You know," he insisted. "Pam's putting the pressure on you, right? Don't worry, women get like that when they smell a wedding in the air."

"What? You trippin'."

"Mm-hm. I might be trippin', but I ain't the one about to be on lockdown."

I came from behind the desk, grabbed Julius by the arm and kindly escorted him to the door. "Time to go. I got work to do."

"Whatever. I'm outta here anyway. Just know that when the pressure get to its boiling point, I'll be here for you, dawg."

"I know, I know. But for now, I got work." I pushed him out the door. Before I reached the desk, Julius stuck his head back in the office. I paused.

"Oh, we got a project on the plate sauteed in your name. You better hurry catching up. Another road trip might be in the works."

"You joking?"

"Nope. I thought I'd pull your coat." A frustrated gasp escaped me. "Thanks."

"No problem. Holla."

"Just what I needed," I mumbled as I dropped into my seat behind the desk.

I had just returned to ATL and wasn't particularly looking forward to leaving again so soon. I had hoped that Julius was mistaking, however, shortly after five, Winthrop, himself, summoned me to his office and began pushing fat imported cigars at me and singing praise. Although I'm not an avid cigar smoker, I joined him. It's always been to my benefit to allow Pam's dad to dominate conversations. In doing so I discovered that he's been one to surround himself with smart and talented business minds to make up for his own incompetence. I eyed my Bulova and wondered why I would have believed that the summons I had received would only take a few moments. It's already taken forty. And I still hadn't accomplished my goal — to say that I didn't want to return to Philly until I caught up on work.

Winthrop twirl the huge cigar between thick lips and tote. He let loose a plume of smoke, scissored the cigar, and pointed. "Wesley, this corporation has been built on sacrifices. Not a lot of employees have left the company since its formulation. Hell, many of the most loyal now hold Board positions and stock, a share of the company's wealth." He stood and began pacing the penthouse office fingered expensive artifacts as he passed them. "My hope is to one day be able to pass down Winthrop's majority shares with the satisfaction of knowing that its interests will be upheld."

"Sir, I'm sure that won't be a problem. There are plenty of competent individuals on the board to choose from."

He paused at a huge, gold-framed oil painting of himself, Mrs. Winthrop, and Pam. "It still isn't the same as if Winthrop's interests remain in the bloodline." He turned and eyed me. "Understand?" he added.

"A heir?"

He shined pearly whites. "Now you do understand my dilemma."

"Of course. You worked hard to build your corporation and you'd like to keep it in the family."

He returned to the desk and stubbed out his cigar. "Absolutely. There's no harm in that, right?"

"Of course not, sir."

"Then, how can I?" His eyes were glued to mine. It was here that I realized that he was referring to Pam wanting a child.

I kept my thoughts to myself and my anger in check. It was obvious that Pam's wanting a child was more for her father's benefit than for the sake of our relationship. Pam's prints were all over this meeting.

"Wesley, I'm sure your loyalty won't ever have to be tested. Am I right, son?"

I felt myself slowly nodding. I'd been backed against a wall. His signifying was enough to assure that my future with the company goes hand in hand with his family's happiness, marriage to Pam, a grandchild whom he can groom to take over the business by the time he's ready to retire.

I had managed to escape what I hope wouldn't become my father-in law's office only having smoked one cigar. The portfolio of Cam-Games' marketing plan was tucked beneath my armpit, and despite my resolve, I was headed back to Philly. Winthrop had called my wanting-to-be-back-home-awhile excuse pure bologna.

At home, I explained it all to Pam. She seemed just as disappointed over me having to return to Philly as I was, only instead of her anger being targeted at her father, who was sending me, it was directed at me.

We were in our bedroom and I was about to lay out a third suit when Pam snatched it from my hands.

"No! Tell him no, Wesley!" she demanded. "He can find somebody else to do it!"

"It's not that simple, Pam. I brought this account to the company. It's a trust thing. It takes time strategizing, putting together marketing plans. You know that. You've been through this exact thing when you began your business."

Pam stood enticingly in a silver Victoria Secret nightie that barely hung across her hips. Her nipples protruded like a second set of eyes and her chest bounced with her fury. She slung the suit back into the closet, on the floor. "I don't care! No, Wesley! We need our time, too. You just left me here a whole week by myself, and now I got to go through that all over again?"

I stopped packing and sat on the bed. "Pam, you can always come with me, you know?"

She sat beside me and huffed. "I can't."

We sat in silence. I was almost convinced that Pam's thoughts were as mine. We'd been drifting apart, nearing the point where neither of us could possibly feel secure about our future together as a couple.

I continued my packing. When I was done, Pam and I walked to the front door, hand in hand. We kissed. While leaving, I turned back to see a solemn Pam wedged against the doorframe, watching me. She waved and blew me a kiss, made me feel as if I were going off to war on another continent. I gave her a reassuring smile and kept stepping. She could thank her father for our misery.

CHAPTER 14

FELICIA

I lay struggling to clear the fuzzy images before me. Every one of my body parts seemed to ache as if I'd spent the last day wrestling hungry gorillas instead of going through routine medical tests. Slowly, my vision returned to normal and the pain in my limbs subsided a bit. The sedative I'd been given had begun to wear off and its effects couldn't have me anymore drained. I rolled from my side onto my back and was surprised to see Miss Shavers at my bedside, buried in a book. I took a deep breath.

"Hey, sleepy head," she greeted.

I cleared my throat and cringed at its rawness. "Hi, Miss Shavers," I croaked.

"Honey, I'm Miss Shavers during school hours. This is hardly school. Call me Carol." She was smiling. "How you feeling?"

"Sore."

She set her paperback down.

"How long you been here?" I asked.

"A couple of hours."

I rubbed my belly and eyed my and the baby's heartbeats on a monitor beside the bed. Thank God my baby's okay, I thought.

"Some of your friends stopped by a while ago. You were sleep, so they said they'll 'get back' later."

I wondered if she were referring to Peaches and Celeste or if Hasim had come by also. I didn't question her. I couldn't muster the strength. Instead, I laid rewinding all that had happened, including the white-haired doctor's words about Connie. "She didn't make it," he had informed me. Those few words alone had been enough to send me on tilt and be sedated. That was yesterday between the many tests. I turned to face Carol. "Do they know what's wrong with me?" I asked.

"Nothing's wrong with you. You had an anxiety attack. The tests were just to make sure that the baby is fine." Her smile was warm and genuine.

"Don't nobody stay in no hospital because they fainted," I challenged.

"Well, not everyone experienced all that you had either." Carol lifted a shopping bag from beside her chair. "Anyway, I picked up a few things for you." She pulled a cotton sweatsuit from the bag. "I spoke with the doctor and he says it's all right if you leave today. I didn't know your size, so this'll have to do til' later."

I didn't know if leaving was good or bad news. I was content just to lay in the hospital bed and not have to face the blow that life's given me. Where would I go? How will I be able to deal with Connie and my mother's deaths?

I fingered the clothes Carol had laid in my lap and tried clearing my mind of everything, tried to simply leave my mind blank, but Connie's lifeless image, collapsed on the sidewalk, just wouldn't leave. Images of how my mother might've been killed also haunted me. I cringed at how brutal my mother's death might've been.

"You okay?" Carol asked.

I nodded.

"I guess, I really can't expect you to be. It's time to be strong."

"I'll be okay."

"I'm sure you will."

We were silent. I wished she'd say something.

"Listen…" she said finally. "How about if you come and stay with me for a while?"

"What?"

"Don't be surprised. I know it's irregular but considering the circumstances."

"I can't do that."

"Why? Where else would you go? With what's his face?"

I stared at the dull, green window shades.

"Felicia, don't let your pride misguide you. It's fine. For right now, let's worry about the child. We all need a little help every now and then. When I was pregnant, at thirteen, someone helped me." She touched my hand. "Let me return the favor, okay?"

I felt tears building behind my eyes. There hasn't been many adults in my life who've shown much concern about my welfare. It's always been me caring about me. There was nothin I could do to keep myself from crying. Deep sobs began escaping me as Connie's image again filled my mind.

The drive from the hospital was uneventful. I felt like a child for the first time in a long while. Having to have someone take care of me felt awful, and Carol had barely spoken three sentences while we were on the road. I got the impression that she was trying to figure me out, probably wondering if I would go over the edge and do something crazy to harm myself.

We reached Carol's Germantown home after a half an hour drive. Inside, Carol grabbed the shopping bag from my hand and ushered me into the living room. "Don't act shy. Come on in and relax."

Carol's home was nothing like I had imagined. It wasn't cold and formal as I'd expected; instead, it was lived-in and cluttered. Children's clothes and jackets were tossed over the backs of chairs along with bookbags and toppled shoes haphazard across the floor. What surprised me most was Jay-Z's latest hit booming from speakers somewhere upstairs in the house. In the dining room, two small girls were lounging on the floor, playing a video game. "Hi, Mommy," they sang one after the other I recognized both from the King center where I had taken Connie. They're eyes spun from the television to me.

I waved hello.

"Hi," they chirped.

Carol introduced us all then headed towards the music I planted myself on the sofa and watched the twins finish their game. The music stopped and a minute later, I heard a steady hum coming from the stairs. Carol arrived downstairs first, and behind her was a teenage boy in a wheelchair. "This is Kevin," Carol announced.

Kevin and I waved hello. Because he was a few years older than me, I wondered if Carol had told him about my situation, about Connie and my mother's deaths, or just that I'll be staying with them. I was uncomfortable, nonetheless. One place I never want to be is in the way. I could have easily gone to stay with Hasim, but that idea didn't sit right with me, especially since he hasn't deeply committed himself to our relationship. I wasn't that naive to believe in his faithfulness. I'd made my decision in the car that I'd at least see what Carol's intentions were before reacting irrationally.

"Are you hungry?" Carol asked. "After two days of hospital foods, I remember being ready to feed on rubber tires and ketchup."

"A little."

"Chile, please, you always talking about 'A little.' Feel free to help yourself. There's plenty."

Kevin rolled by me. "Come on. I'll show you where everything's at."

I followed Kevin into the kitchen. Carol had been right.

The refrigerator was full. There was so much to choose from, unlike what I was used to. We decided on frozen pizzas and Dipsy Doodles. Kevin put enough in the microwave for his sisters, too.

"So, what's your story?" Kevin asked. We were at the kitchen table. His question pulled my eyes away from the fake, caged parrot in the corner.

"My story?"

"Yeah. How come you're here?"

"Your mom never told you?"

"Nope. Just that you'll be staying here." He began filling four glasses with ice cubes from a tray.

"I don't really want to talk about it," I replied.

"You sure?"

"Yeah. I'm sure."

We were silent for a few minutes until the "ding" of the microwave interrupted. "Pizza up!" Kevin called as if my brushing off his question didn't matter. He pulled the pizzas from the microwave. "My mom never brings strangers to the house, so you must be in some kinda trouble or something," he said matter-of-factly.

"I'm not in any trouble."

"Is it because you're pregnant?"

"Do you always ask so many questions?"

Kevin bit into his pizza and smiled. "Yep." He called for the twins again.

I munched and looked on as the twins squabbled over whether they'll sit at the kitchen table, how sloppy the other eats, and how they get on one another's nerves. Carol came in, having changed into sweats and poured herself a glass of orange juice. She took a swig then eyed me. "I put most of Kia's things in Kelly's room. When you're ready, you can go upstairs and rest or whatever."

"Aw, Mommy!" Kia cried.

"Girl, hush. You sleep with me anyway."

Kelly giggled. "'Cause she a scaredy cat."

"I am not!"

"Are too."

"Am not!"

"Mm-hm."

"Okay, girls. Don't be showing off."

Upstairs, Carol showed me which room was Kia's. The room was comfortable enough. A twin bed. Mickey Mouse wall papering. A small dresser in one corner matching the rust color carpet.

I had no use for storage space and things like such, so just knowing that I had a place to lay my head was sufficient enough for me. I laid back on the bed and rubbed my swollen belly.

No matter how hard I tried not thinking about their deaths, Connie and my mother's images wouldn't go away. I don't think they ever will. I've never felt so empty and alone.

It had never mattered how bad things had gotten for me at home, I had always known that Connie was there to give me fulfillment and purpose. And now that she's gone, I had no idea how my life will turn without her. I couldn't help but allow the tears to flow. I tried wrestling back the deep sobs that were escaping me but couldn't. I tried even harder when there was a knock on the bedroom door. It was Carol, asking if I were all right.

I wiped my tears and answered, "Yes."

She didn't enter.

When I believed that she had walked away, I curled into a ball and cried some more.

CHAPTER 15

CAROL

Students' files were stacked a foot high on my desk, two feet high on the floor, and another stack occupied the straight back beside my desk. I glanced around the shambled office. Every drawer of my file cabinet had needed reorganizing, but only after each student's file had been reviewed and categorized according to those needing immediate attention.

There was so much to do, and yet, my thoughts continuously wandered back to an earlier call I'd made to Child Services to explore the consequences, if any, of what could happen if I declined being Felicia's temporary guardian.

The woman I spoke with had confirmed my notions. Felicia would almost certainly be placed in foster care and, once her child is born, the child, too, would become a product of the system until Felicia is eighteen and capable of being a "suited mother," as the woman had so boldly put it.

While the woman spoke, so much of my childhood had flashed before me. She'd made it seem all too routine, made me nearly zip lock my original idea to say nothing; however, I'd already taken a huge risk on Felicia by signing her release from jail and felt obligated to know the alternative. Although I never intended to become emotionally involved in Felicia's life, I have. But, until her mother and sister are buried, and she's gotten over the shock of it all, I feel the least I could do is provide her food and shelter. Just like I explained to Felicia before dropping her off at her doctor's appointment this morning, the decision whether she stays, or leaves is hers. I'm willing to try and be a mentor for her in a lot of ways, but I already have enough to deal with raising my own three children and am not in the position or can foresee the patience needed to deal with the immature decisions she's making. All I asked of her is to give us the time we'll need to develop a level of trust.

Forty-five minutes later, after I had cleared the desk of files and was skimming through the stack on the floor, my office door opened. My jaw dropped when I saw who was entering. It was James, my twins' father.

James has always had a way of gnawing at my soul, sucking and clinging onto me like a hungry tick. I sat frozen.

"Hey, boo," he croaked.

I blinked a few times to assure myself that I wasn't dreaming. "What...what the...why are you here?" I stammered.

He grinned. "You."

My eyebrow rose. "Oh yeah? Why's that?"

He closed the door. "I wanted to see you."

"For what?"

"Can I just visit?"

I rested back in my chair and took in his shabbiness.

He was puny in his cotton warm-up suit, and his face was sunken. He crossed over to the desk, smiling.

"It depends on why you're here," I answered.

"I was on my way to a meeting and thought I'd drop by. See how you're settling in with the new gig and all." He surveyed the office. "Kinda messy ain't it?"

"It's called working, something you need to get back to so that your daughters can get to college."

"Whoa! Hold up, Carol. I'm not here to beg or argue. I just wanted to say hello and let you know that I'm still alive."

"That's a relief. Now bye."

James and I had been in an up and down, twelve-year relationship. Unfortunately, he'd found another love to replace me and his sense of family responsibility. Crack cocaine. James' refusal to stop getting high had tested my patience to capacity and had eventually become the last straw. I had given him my maximum effort, and, in return, he had still chosen drugs.

My eyes followed his scrawny frame ease into a chair. "Come on, don't be like that."

I stood and grabbed a handful of folders from the chair. "Be like what, James? We have nothing to talk about." I began putting files away.

"We go too far back to be at each other's throat."

"Coulda fooled me." I spun to face him. "What is it, James? You want to see the girls?"

"Among other things."

"Other things?"

"Well, yeah."

I returned to my task and he came to stand beside me.

"I want us to all go out somewhere…try to, you know…be a family again."

"Not likely."

He looked disappointed. "You not even gonna consider it?"

I slammed shut the file drawer and grabbed another stack of files. I couldn't believe that James was still chasing the dream that he'd turned his back on, the dream that I had once been so willing to fight for. I was pissed and waved a folder toward him. "You know, James…you are really a piece of work. When we were together, you made it clear that we weren't a priority in your life. Now you standing here, after having done lied, cheated, and stole from us, and say that you've changed. Well, let me tell you something: we're doing just fine without your bullshit. Just fine. So, for all of our sakes, why don't you just go? Work on yourself. Because you aren't fooling anybody right now."

He sighed, "It's like that?"

I stared directly into his coal-black eyes. "It's exactly like that. Now, I'd appreciate it if you left so that I can get some work done."

He licked his charred lips the way he used to when he was trying to put his Mack down. "Okay. I see ain't much change with you." He started toward the door, obviously disappointed. But I didn't care. He'd dogged me enough with his sorry ass excuses and tired-behind apologies.

I reached the file cabinet and went about my work as if he weren't even in the office. I felt him staring at me while he stood at the open door. I refused to look his way. Only after the door was shut did I look up. James was gone. "Oh well," I mumbled then filed the next folder.

Mentally, I was beat up. My head was aching from an afternoon of devising ways to approach some of the students' problems which I read about. From what I'd read in their files, counseling is only a small fraction of their needs. Many of their problems stem from their family settings, and unless more parents become involved in the children's lives, there's not much I'll be able to do for them.

My workday ended an hour later than usual. To add to my frustrations, traffic would not let up the entire drive home. I was kicking myself for having had stayed the main route the entire ride, then again, just knowing that Felicia's situation was at the house waiting on me kind of enticed me to relish the time to gather my thoughts.

I pulled the Nissan in front of the house and grabbed the handful of files I'd brought home to review. I hadn't cleared the doorway before Kia and Kelly were at me, flashing white strips of paper.

"Sign this for me, Mommy?" Kia pestered.

"I asked first," Kelly whined.

"Can you wait until I at least get in the house?" I grabbed the papers from their fingers and slipped the folders on to the sofa. "Where's Kevin?" I asked.

"On his computer," answered Kelly.

"And Felicia?"

"Upstairs," both answered. They were hoping around as if there were hot coals beneath their feet.

I began reading the papers. Their school was planning a field trip to the Franklin Institute in a week.

"Mommy, that girl crazy," Kia blurted.

I looked up from my reading, "why do you say that?"

"Cause she is."

"Did she do something crazy?"

Kia nodded.

"All she do is cry," Kelly added.

I fished a pen from my handbag and signed the slips. "Has she been upstairs all day?"

They both nodded.

I pointed to the jackets and bookbags tossed across the sofa's back. "Can ya'll take those things upstairs where they belong?" I asked.

As I climbed the stairs, I wondered if the twins had paid my request any mind. Probably not. They were too busy yelping and hooraying over their trip to the Franklin Institute. I looked in on Kevin first. His door was ajar, and he was at his computer. computer. "Busy?" I asked.

"Kinda." He never turned from the computer screen.

Kevin's room was a mess, much as it has always been throughout his childhood. The bed was half made, dresser-top cluttered with cosmetics, clothes, a single Nike. A dumbbell lie half covered in blue jean near the closet, and two mountains of books were stacked beneath the single un-curtained window.

I stood behind him and ran my fingers across the wave pattern in his hair. "What are you working on?"

"My resume'."

"Okay. You go, boy. You trying to save me some money when you start school?"

He blushed. "Not really."

I popped him upside the head.

"Ow! I'm just joking."

"Did you check on Felicia like I asked you to?"

"Been busy. Anyway, she came from the doctor and locked herself in the room."

"You've been busy, huh?"

He pointed to the computer screen. "Look how much I got done."

I scanned the text on the screen. "You should list job experiences in chronological order," I suggested, "...and development has no 'e' after the 'p'...and..."

"Okay, Mom, that's enough. I'll let you read it when it's done."

"Good. If I know you, you'd probably say the heck with it and not change a thing."

"I promise."

"I'm going to hold you to that, too."

"Don't I know it." He smiled up at me.

I left Kevin to his work and knocked on Felicia's door before entering. She was lying belly-up, staring at the ceiling. "Hey, you. You okay?"

She sat up and sniffled, tried to mask the fact that she'd been crying. "I'm fine."

"You sure? You don't seem fine." I sat beside her. "You know it's all right to grieve?"

"I'm okay."

"Have you eaten?"

"No."

"Do you intent to?"

"Nooo," Felicia whined before bursting into tears.

I hugged her and tried to give the comfort I knew she needed. I was unsure if I had enough hugs to ease her pain because she was crying as if she'd been scared throughout her lifetime.

It had taken an hour and some serious comforting to calm Felicia down and convince her that taking care of herself means taking care of her baby. I realized that my pleas had skipped and stalled like a scratched record and it was difficult having to continuously repeat the exact message; however, this time, I believe that my points have reached her.

We were seated at the kitchen table, feasting on fried chicken and mushy rice that Kevin had prepared. The twins were bickering about the field trip, and Kevin was browsing through a Source magazine while Felicia and I picked at our food.

"I'm going in town tomorrow if you'd like to come?" I asked Felicia.

"Oooh! I wanna go, Mommy," Kia chimed.

"I'm talking to Felicia, Kia."

Kia poked out her lips.

"You game?"

Felicia continued picking at her rice then shrugged. "I'll go."

"Good. I was thinking that we could pick up a few things for you."

She nodded, but I got the impression that she'd agreed simply out of necessity more-so than anything else.

The Galley was packed with shoppers, as packed as I've ever seen it. Regardless of every twist and turn I made to avoid bumping into another person, I continuously did. Children were giggling while rushing to their next adventure. Felicia and I were carrying one shopping bag each mostly clothes and shoes for Felicia. I knew that the twins would have a hissy fit if I didn't pick them up an outfit or two, so I bought the twins matching skirt-sets and Kevin two sweaters.

We were nearing Footlockers when Felicia abruptly stopped. "What's wrong?" I asked.

She only stared, caused my eyes to follow hers. Hasim and two other teenage boys were exiting a store, heading our way. As much as I wanted to yank Felicia inside of a store and hide her, I didn't. I slowed my pace instead and wondered what was on Felicia's mind. Her sudden pace indicated to me that she was going to attempt to walk by him, but he'd spotted us. Hasim seemed pleased to see Felicia and was even considerate enough to give me a glancing over. He'd stopped in Felicia's path. "Damn, boo, where you been? I been tryna holla."

She stepped around him.

He grabbed her wrist. "Whoa, whoa, whoa. Whassup?"

"Ain't nothin up, Hasim." Felicia's face was determined.

"Excuse me," I said, "can we take care of our business, please?"

Hasim eyed me. "Ain't you that counselor chick?"

"No. I'm no chick."

"Right. I got you. My bad. How you doing?"

"Fine. Thank you. We do have somewhere to go, though."

His eyes were back on Felicia.

"I only need a minute."

"But…"

"It's cool," Felicia interrupted. "Let 'em talk."

I stepped aside and watched Felicia's eyes roll in their sockets while Hasim spoke. His boys stood aside as I did, looking on. Hasim's lips were pumping high octane in effort to keep up with Felicia's rolling eyes. Back and forth their conversation was going. I rehashed similar scenarios with James.

The argument, the apology, the caresses, then James' glee at how quickly I had come to "my" senses and had accepted the promises that he had made to me. Back then, I had pretty much conceded that things, more than likely, would never change for the betterment of our relationship, but just out of pure fear of possible loneliness and abandonment, I had caved to his weeded words. Back then, I had never wanted to raise my children alone, and it has taken years for me to rediscover myself.

When I returned from my thoughts, Hasim was tracing a finger across Felicia's cheek and her eyes were no longer disinterested, they were locked on to Hasim. Her demeanor had changed in just those few moments. She seemed to be puddy in his thuggish hands. I became concerned and interrupted them. "Excuse me. Are you ready to go, Felicia?"

"In a minute," she answered testily.

"Uh-uh. I'm ready now." I stepped between them. "You all can finish this conversation another time," I told them. "Let's go."

"Who you think you is, lady?" Hasim asked.

I kept my back to Hasim and my eyes on Felicia, who wouldn't look at me but at the ground.

"Can't you see she coming home with me, lady?" asked Hasim.

"No. I can't," I shot back, my stare never wavering from Felicia. I pulled her aside. "Girl, what's wrong with you? Can't you see that this boy is nothing but trouble?"

"Miss Shavers, you don't even know Hasim."

I turned her face toward me. "I'm 'Miss Shavers' again, huh? And for your information, yes, I do. I've dealt with thugs just like him my entire life. All he's concerned about is using you for his gain. Not respecting you."

"You don't understand," she pleaded.

"I don't understand what, Felicia. How he's going to leave the drug game and be a real father to your baby?"

"He will."

"When Felicia? When?" I realized my voice was beginning to rise and also that Felicia's decision had to be her own.

I'm not this child's mother, I thought. But even so, I felt solely responsible for her well-being. I stepped back and took her in, shook my head. "Don't do this, Felicia. Don't ruin your life over this guy. He doesn't love you, chile."

"How do you know!?" she shouted. "How could you know!? You don't know me!" Tears had begun forming in her eyes. "All you know is that I somehow remind you of you. Pregnant and alone. But somebody loves me, and you just hate that, don't you?" She slung the shopping bag to my feet. "I don't need your charity!"

I watched her stomp around me and into Hasim's awaiting arms, left me staring at his smug-ass snarl as he escorted her away. Mrs. Burns had been right, I thought.

I was too involved.

CHAPTER 16

WESLEY

I was grateful that my flight to Philly had taken off as scheduled. It had been a test of willpower to just sit in the airport and wait, let alone, try to deal with having to leave home again. If there had been a delay in the flight's schedule, I might've reconsidered altogether. Then again, like always when something needs doing, it's been me to step up to the plate and handle whatever that something was.

I stretched out in my seat and closed my eyes, tried to remember when I last had a vacation, the last time that I truly had a relaxing stretch without pressure to do anything other than enjoy myself for weeks on end. It's been a while — a long while.

"Can I get you anything, sir?" a flight attendant asked, interrupting my thoughts.

"No. Thank you."

She was Caucasian, slim in build with an exquisite smile. Her smile reminded me of Carol's. Suddenly, my apprehensions of returning to Philly settled a bit. When the flight attendant moved on, I again shut my eyes and embraced the memories of when Carol and I had made love.

Although it's been years ago; nonetheless, those sweet memories still cling to my soul.

Carol's scent. Her warmth. The way she had murmured my name. My visions were as vivid as if our lovemaking had occurred this morning. I shivered, tried to envision farther back to our first kiss. Before I could reach my destination, Pam's image interrupted. Nagging. Pressuring. Demanding. Then the marketing presentation interrupted the thoughts of Pam. I opened my eyes. It was useless.

It surprised me that there weren't more passengers aboard the flight to Philly. I obeyed the "FASTEN YOUR SEATBELTS" light, shut my eyes, and unleashed my visions of Carol. She and I could've been something special. And although being with Carol had meant accepting a ready-made family, I'd been prepared to accept those responsibilities. Still today, I feel comfortable accepting those terms, and knowing that she's still single, and from what I saw of her, she's still as lovely and alluring as ever.

Again, my eyes popped open. This time, Pam's image was shouting obscenities at me for cheating on her, caused me to shift in my seat and peer around at the somber faces scattered throughout the plane's cabin. I grabbed my briefcase when the plane leveled off and began preparing my presentation. I wondered if my infatuation with Carol is clue enough that a committed relationship with Pam will never be possible. It seems clear that Pam will always, in my heart, hold second to Carol. Should pursue Carol? I asked myself. With all those emotions that I have for her bottled inside of me, I wondered if pursuing Carol again would be wise. But I'd have to, need to, and intend to. Regardless of what my conscience was telling me, my heart was saying otherwise.

Once my flight arrived in Philly, I caught a taxi to the DoubleTree. The weather outside was gray and humid, but inside the hotel's lobby was cool and brightly lit. I checked myself in then tipped the bellboy handsomely to escort my baggage to my room before I headed back outside.

Evening was coming on fast by the time I finally reached Magic's house. I had to ring the doorbell twice then bang on the door three times before he finally answered. He stood in the doorway half-dressed with a confused look in his eyes.

"You plan on letting me in?" I asked him. "Boy, I thought you was back in Georgia?"

"I was. Now, I'm here again."

He still hadn't stepped aside, just stood there fiddling with the leather belt dangling from his checkered slacks and twirling the gray hairs on his flabby chest. His attention seemed elsewhere behind him.

"Am I interrupting something?"

"Nah. Hell nah. Come on in."

"You sure?"

"Yeah, yeah. Come on in here." He stepped aside and I followed him into the living room, took a seat on the black leather sofa.

"So, why you back in town so quick?"

"Business."

"Need somewhere to crash?"

"Nope. I'm setup downtown already. Company expense. I do need to borrow the car though."

He gazed toward the stairs. "Yeah. Sure. Let me get the keys for you."

Magic had added on a few pounds over the years. He resembled a Chinese Buddha, and his receding hairline gave him a comical appearance. He hurried up the stairs. I heard a female's voice cut through the quietness of the house then Magic's footsteps returning.

"Got company?" I teased when he was back downstairs.

"Not really. Gloria stopped by for a sec." He was winded.

"Mm-hm."

"Yeah. We…uhm…gotta uh, plan something 'bout the shop."

"Yeah? Like what?"

"Uhm…you know, the painting' and things I tol' you 'bout a long time ago." He finished stumbling through his lie before tossing the car's keys over to me. It was obvious that he was trying to get back to his business upstairs by the way he rocked on his heels.

"Alright, Unc. I got you."

He blushed.

"I'm glad you and Gloria are working things out."

He nodded and started toward the door. "Just drop the keys in the mail slot when you're done, okay?"

"No problem," I replied, taking clue.

We shook hands at the door.

"I'll see you later, Gloria!" I hollered upstairs.

"Bye, Wesley!" she called back.

I smiled at Magic who was shaking his head. "You know you ain't right, boy?"

"I know. But I couldn't resist."

Magic's Caddy was parked a few doors down from the house.

Before pulling off, I browsed through his CDs and settled on the Stylistics. I was in a hurry to go nowhere in particular, so I drove around the old neighborhood just to take in a few sights. Not much had changed.

I turned off of Norris Street on to 32nd then headed down Montgomery to 33rd.

Fairmount Park was just as I remembered; although, the recreation center's basketball courts had received a face lift and several stone benches had been placed around the area.

I cruised by Septa's bus barn and headed passed Strawberry Mansion High, crooning to "Betcha Bye Golly Wow." I took Susquehanna all the way to 22nd Street, passed Raymond Rosen projects. Every one of the twelve story buildings had been imploded and two-story rowhomes had been placed where the huge monuments once stood.

As I passed William Dick Elementary School, I pulled the Caddy over and parked in what had once been "my spot." It was the place where I had once found so much inspiration and had sought out change for my soul.

I turned off the car's stereo and sat reminiscing.

Regardless of my few accomplishments, I still feel like I hadn't done everything possibly needed in order to rectify my wrongs.

I'd been fortunate to establish a career, a home, and financial stability, but my soul still seems to crave. Images of "what could have been" filled my head. Images of Carol and myself.

I started the car and pulled off. I'd already made up my mind about what needs to be done, what was missing in my life. It was love. I needed to see Carol and try my hand at convincing her that we can get passed our tribulations. It might be crazy of me to assume, but I wholeheartedly feel that Carol might be willing to forgive me for my betrayal.

CHAPTER 17

CAROL

The school's halls were empty of students and the "click clacking" of my shoes resented throughout the hall's emptiness. I passed by lockers and closed classroom doors with my mind preoccupied. Occasionally, a student would emerge, pass by me and I'd say hello, but still my thoughts remained elsewhere, concerns over the funeral of Felicia's mother and sister that Felicia, herself, hadn't attended. Then again, I had only stayed for a brief time paying my respects; however, I had assumed, if Felicia had attended, that she would have been present throughout the entire service.

It was difficult deciding if I would attend the service at all. I had needed to see Felicia and felt somewhat obligated to be there in support of her. I have to admit that not seeing her there was a true disappointment.

I opened my office door and was surprised by a large basket of white and red roses centered on my desk. I plucked the card from them and read:

Dearest Carol,

My thoughts are and have always been with you. I'm remembering you…loving you…
Wesley

I inhaled the roses, remembering just as Wesley's card indicated he'd been doing. It's been such a long time since I've found comfort in a man's arms. More than six years. Needing to be with a man, surprisingly, hasn't been a priority in my life. It only surprises me because I had once believed that I needed a man in my life. But, since then, between earning my degrees and raising my children, there hasn't been time to focus on a relationship and because of my commitment towards independence, so many lonely nights have passed with my face buried in my pillow, feeling as if my being alone was entirely my fault. Over time, I realized that my failed relationships hadn't been my fault alone. Langston had been killed, James had turned to drugs, and Wesley was discovered to be someone with an unforgiving past that I couldn't find the willingness to forgive. It's said that time heals all wounds and, maybe so, because having seen Wesley recently has stirred up all of those lonely emotions which I've been running from all of these years.

I dropped into my desk chair and stared at the basket of flowers before slapping it off of the desk and into the wastebasket. I wasn't so angry at the idea of Wesley sending me flowers. I was angry at men in general, especially at Hasim for interfering in Felicia's life during a time when she's so vulnerable.

I reluctantly pulled the basket of flowers from the wastebasket and set them back on the desk, thought about who'd actually set them there, Mr. Epps or Mrs. Burns. Or, had Wesley put them there himself.

Later, during lunch, after having been on edge most of the morning, I searched the sea of young faces and listened to some of the vulgarity spewing from their mouths. Just what I needed, I thought.

Another reason to feel like the job I've set out to do was unachievable. I grabbed a tray of tossed salad and took my usual seat across from Mrs. Burns. I was still surveying the cafeteria.

"Looking for someone?" Mrs. Burns asked.

"Huh? Not really," I lied.

"Mm-hm. Who did what?"

"No one did anything. I was just wondering if Felicia Knight showed up for class that's all."

"The pregnant child whose mother and sister passed; you mean?"

I paused a second. "You know her?"

"Of course, I know her. I make it my business to know every student."

I drenched my salad in French dressing and surveyed the room some more.

"You can stop searching, Carol. She's not here. Hasn't been to classes all week."

I stared at Mrs. Burns' makeup job. She looked ancient while shoving a forkful of mashed potatoes into her mouth. "All week?" I asked.

She nodded.

I wanted to shout how I had driven Felicia to and from school for two days. But I hadn't told Mrs. Burns anything about how I've been personally involved in Felicia's life and wasn't about to give her ammunition to chew me out.

"Are you prepared for the faculty meeting this afternoon?" asked Mrs. Burns, interrupting my thoughts.

"I didn't answer.

"Are you all right, chile?" she added.

"Yeah. I'm fine," I mumbled still stunned. "Excuse me a moment?" I asked, rising from my seat.

The students sat around the cafeteria in groups of females and males. The females were at their norm and sat at the far end of the lunchroom while the male students were at the opposite end. I recognized one girl as a friend of Felicia's and approached her. She looked up at me with curious eyes.

"Can I speak with you for a minute?" I asked.

She pointed at herself. "Who? Me?"

"Yes. You," I answered.

"For what?" She looked as if I were there to punish her.

I stepped back a bit while she slowly rose then guided her out of earshot of her girlfriends. "Where's Felicia?" I asked.

"What Felicia?"

I smiled. "What's your name?" I asked.

"Celeste Watts."

"Celeste, Felicia isn't in trouble or anything. I just need to speak with her. She hasn't been in school lately."

"I don't know where she at. I haven't seen her."

"What about Hasim?"

"What about 'em?"

"Have you seen him?"

"No."

"Can you at least tell me where Hasim lives?"

"Why you wanna know that for?"

"Because I'm trying to help Felicia through some really rough times is all."

She turned away from me, obviously aware of Felicia's family deaths. Her expression saddened. "Don't tell nobody I tol' you, okay?"

"I won't. I promise you."

She sucked her teeth. "He live in Richard Allen…at least his sister do."

I've been familiar with Richard Allen project for years. Janice, James' mother, also lives there and I've lived there as a teen. I got Hasim's sister's address from Celeste and saw that it was only a block from Janice's rowhome.

The faculty meeting could not have ended soon enough for me. Although I had focused on the school's curriculum, my thoughts wandered in anticipation of getting where I needed to be at the meeting's conclusion.

I pulled the car in front of the address that Celeste had given me and stepped out into the cool evening air. I contemplated whether what I was doing would give me any relief but knowing that I at least gave an effort to reach out to Felicia, during this crucial time, couldn't leave me feeling any worse.

I entered the rowhome and climbed the stairs to the second floor with my heart pacing twice as fast. It's been a long time since I've felt so nervous, not since I had taken my college SATs.

A slim woman answered my knock. She fingered a blue headwrap while eyeing me. "Yes?"

I cleared my throat. "Hi. I'm Carol Shavers, a counselor at Girls' High. Is Felicia Knight here?"

She rolled her tongue over bucked teeth and looked me up and down. "Why you lookin' for 'er?"

"I need to speak with her."

Behind the woman were two small children on a sofa, playing a video game. She peered over her opposite shoulder of the children then stepped aside. "Felicia, some woman at the door" she called before walking away without inviting me inside.

I sighed in relief of having found Felicia so quickly, however, when Felicia arrived at the door, she rolled her eyes.

"What now?" she gasped.

"I came to talk."

"About what?" She folded her arms across her chest, causing her belly to swell forward.

"About you."

We stood a few moments eyeing one another. She, too, stepped away from the door without inviting me in. I stepped inside.

The small living room was cluttered with too much furniture for the small space. Felicia stood beside a set of tricycles, looking through me, I felt. "I hope you not here to preach," she spat.

I smiled to ease the tension. "Not exactly."

"Then what?"

I had carried my briefcase with me and set it on the floor.

From an adjoining room, the slim girl, who I guessed to be Hasim's sister, was eavesdropping.

"Felicia, I came because I'm worried about you."

"Well, I'm fine."

"I can see that, but I can't help the way I feel."

"Well, I am."

"Then why haven't you been to classes?"

She circled behind me and struggled into a chair. "I didn't feel like it."

"That's why I'm here."

"Not to preach?"

I shook my head. "Not to preach, Felicia, but to ask you to come back to school. I understand how you must feel, but to just —"

"I will. When I'm ready."

We were silent for few moments. I sensed her annoyance and wondered if I should've come in the first place. I told myself that there was no turning back and dove ahead. I kneeled eye to eye with her and grasped her hand. "Are you really fine with quitting school, Felicia?"

She looked away without answering.

"You already know that I had my first child at thirteen, too. I was frightened and bitter because the father wasn't able to be there. He was killed in a car crash. Believe me, I had no idea what I'd do. But somebody helped me through it. Just like I'd like to help you through it."

"Who says I need any help?"

"No one. But it's always good to know that someone is there is all I'm saying."

She snatched her hand from mine and sprung from her seat. "For how long!" she snapped. "Until you decide I'm not worth it no more!"

I stood and watched her eyes begin to water up.

"Until you're sick of me, just like my drunk-ass mother was, and decide I'ma unfit mom!" The tears began to fall as she vented. "All my life people have been tellin' me how worthless I am. How…how much of a little…a little bitch I am." Deep sobs had begun escaping her. "Now you think I'ma believe you! You don't even know me! You don't care about my baby like you say. You only care about…about making yourself feel better by rescuing some poor project girl!"

I looked away. "That's not true."

"Yes, it is! All you care about is your nice house and preppy kids. So, don't be looking down on me, 'cause I'ma be fine. Me and my baby. So why don't you just leave me alone?"

I looked at the two children who were now watching us. The slim woman had entered the living room and was no longer hiding her interest. I picked up my briefcase. "You're wrong, Felicia. I do care," I managed before turning toward the door.

Before I could reach the door, it burst open and Hasim stormed inside. He was in a panic as he slammed it close behind himself and began fumbling with the locks. "Go in the other room!" he was shouting.

We all stared.

"Go 'head!" he shouted. "Now!"

Before anyone could react, the door burst open again and a man wearing a black ski-mask was inside pointing a huge gun. Everything was moving faster than my mind could register. Shots rang out. Lots of shots. Screams. Curses. Then I saw Hasim holding a gun, too. He was firing shots back at the man and all I could do is stand frozen, too scared to move. I was in shock. Chaos was all around me, still I couldn't grasp the deadliness of what was happening. Then something knocked me to the floor. In seconds, my vision blurred, and the room began spinning. Suddenly, there was nothing before me but total blackness. I could still hear shouts and the children's screaming, but then, even that ceased. And then there was nothing but total darkness.

CHAPTER 18

WESLEY

Drinks were on Winthrop Industries, so I allowed our bar tab to extend beyond my personal preference. Calvin Davis, CEO of Cam-Games, sat across the table from me, doubling up on scotch. We were discussing marketing ideas I had presented at our earlier meeting with Cam-Games' Board of Directors.

The presentation had gone fine, and now I was even more confident, considering the upbeat conversation we've been engaged in. Cam-Games' newly developed doll line was our primary focus.

"I have to admit, Wesley, Winthrop was the first I considered to handle this project," said Calvin. "There aren't many companies as dependable, let alone capable of making the commitment necessary to help Cam-Games develop."

"Thank you. Mr. Davis."

"Cal. Call me Cal since we'll no longer be strangers." I smiled, satisfied.

"Sure. Then Cal it is."

"Good." He threw back a sixth double scotch and smacked thin pink lips.

I guessed Cal's age to be mid-fifties, mostly because of the full head of gray and wrinkled, pale white skin.

"If there's any paperwork necessary to finalize our deal," he began, "I'll have my secretary fax you directly."

I nodded and sipped my fourth rum and Coke. I'd been careful to moderate my drinking. The last thing I wanted was to be perceived as a lush and blow my chance at getting the extension on the account.

A thin, chocolate-skinned waitress approached our table. "Would you gentlemen like another round?"

Cal jovially tapped a round belly and smiled. "No. I'm fine. I believe I've already reached my limit."

She turned toward me.

"I'm fine. Thank you."

"Okay then…" She peeled off our check and laid it on the table, face down.

I peeked at it then handed her a company credit card.

"I guess, since our business has concluded, I'll excuse myself to the restroom," Cal said.

"Certainly."

We stood and shook hands. While doing so, my pager went off.

"An important man," Cal joked before departing.

I checked the pager, didn't recognize the number and headed to a phone.

Madman-like, I turned the Cadillac into Thomas Jefferson Hospital's parking lot. The entire drive over, my mind had been spinning. It felt like my heart would thump clear out of my chest. "I can't believe this!" I yelled as I screeched into a parking spot. I burst through the hospital's doors, mumbling about how unbelievable this was. I bumrushed the attendant's station so panicky that the pudgy woman behind the counter flinched. Beads of sweat had formed across my forehead.

"Can I help you?" asked the attendant.

"Carol Shavers. What room?" My voice shook when I spoke.

I watched her fingers glide across her computer's keyboard then stop.

She smiled up at me. "Miss Shavers is in room 207. Second floor. You can sign the visitors' form here then at the nurses' station up there."

I signed in, thanked the woman, and hustled toward the elevators. As soon as I stepped from the elevator, I saw Kevin at the nurses' station. He noticed me coming and met me halfway.

"What happened?" I asked.

"My mom got shot."

"Shot? By who? Why?"

He shrugged. "Some guy is all I know."

"Is she all right?"

"Her arm and shoulder are messed up."

I started toward room 207, but Kevin grabbed my arm. "She don't know I called you," he warned. "I'm not sure she wanna see you."

I breathed deeply and thought back to the last time she and I were together, her still not forgiving me. "Anybody in there with her now?"

"Uh-uh. The doctor was just giving her some pain medicine and stuff. He said she'll be okay."

"That's a relief." I walked to the door and peeked inside.

Carol was sitting upright with her eyes closed. Her left arm and shoulder were heavily bandaged and in a sling.

"You going in?" Kevin asked.

I nodded.

"Well, I gotta call the house. KK don't know yet. Mom made me promise not to tell 'em."

"That's probably best for now. How about you?"

"What about me?"

"You okay?"

Kevin nodded. "I'ma go make the call," he said then began wheeling himself away.

"Hey Kevin!" I called.

He stopped.

"Why'd you call me?"

He shrugged. "Because I know you care," he simply said then turned away.

I stepped within the coolness of the hospital room, trying to piece together what exactly I could say to persuade Carol not to throw me out on my ass. My steps were measured as not to awaken her, but then, her eyes, those soft brown eyes, opened and I froze halfway to her bedside.

She only stared.

"Hello," I softly said while trying to hide in the room's dimness. I had imagined screams from Carol ordering me to GET OUT! They hadn't come.

She cleared her throat. "What are you doing here?"

I took the chance to smile. "I needed to see a friend. How you feeling?"

"Doped up." A weak smile escaped her.

I took another step forward. "I'm told you can go home later. Good news, huh?"

"Mm-hm. But I just wanna rest."

"Sure. I understand."

"How'd you know anyway?"

"Kevin called me."

"That boy worry too much."

"You did a good job with him. He's really gonna make a difference."

"Hm. Thanks." Carol's words were a tired whisper.

I made my way to the bed and held her hand. I was surprised she allowed me to. Her skin was as soft as I remembered, and I've never felt more bonded with her. Our eyes met, and without warning my soul opened up to her. I couldn't control my trembling. "Carol, I'm so sorry," I began. "For years I've tried to live to make a difference and, somehow, I always feel like it isn't enough."

"Don't, Wesley," she interrupted.

I stopped her. "I need to say this, Carol."

She bit her bottom lip and kept her eyes on mine.

I continued. "My past is exactly that. My past. The boy I was then isn't the man standing beside you today. My heart has changed. I've changed.

"Carol, I dream about us still. I dream about a life with you as my wife. I dream about…about being the best man that I can be." With each word, I felt a calmness, a relief over being able to, finally, face this woman and express myself in all honesty. "So many times, I've thought about whether I'll ever find my soulmate," I continued, "but I know now that she's been there all these years, Carol. It's you who I need in my life. It's you I've been praying for."

Tears had begun welling in Carol's eyes. She squeezed my hand, and before I knew it the words were out. "Carol, will you marry me?"

A single tear fell across her cheek, and I've never seen her look more beautiful. I understood that it was a lot for her to absorb, and her silence revealed that. We were silent for what seemed an eternity. My body tensed as her grip on my hand subsided.

"Don't do this to me, Wesley. Please, not now."

"I know my timing might not be perfect, but I only know how I feel, what I've felt for years."

"I'm sorry, Wesley. I don't think I can. How can I?"

"Easily. Listen, you don't have to answer me now. Just think about it, okay?" I leaned forward and placed a kiss at the corner of her mouth. "You just rest and heal."

After seeing Carol home and returning Magic's car, I arrived back in Atlanta during what had to be the worst traffic jam in the city's history. It had taken me nearly two hours to taxi home. It was all good, though. It gave me time to evaluate my relationship with Pam. I understood the commitment I had made to Carol but was still unsure how to handle Pam's inevitable fireworks as a result of my decision. Everything I had established over the past six years was now in jeopardy. My career especially. However, having proposed to Carol somewhat assured me that everything will work out for the best.

At the apartment, I showered and began my plan of action to deal with Pam, but before I had completed it, I heard the front door to the apartment close. I wrapped myself in a towel and grabbed a second to dry myself with. Pam was calling for me.

"I'm in the bedroom," I answered.

She entered the bedroom, without a hello, and headed straight for the walk-in closet. "I can't believe Mario would pull this shit!" she spat, rummaging through her clothes. She began stripping from a tight t-shirt and a cotton wrap skirt. "He could've booked ten of the top models in the world to work the runway, but his cheap-ass wanna cut corners."

"How much did they want?" I asked.

She paused to stare at me. "That's not the point. If you want results you have to pay for them. Look at the money top designers spend to promote their lines. Millions!"

I pulled on a pair of sweats and thought how callus Pam has always been with money.

"Last year, he promised me. I'll fix his gay ass," she threatened. She exited the closet carrying a long, silk evening gown.

"What's that for?"

"The Baxter's' dinner party is tonight. I was forced to commit to it."

"How can somebody force you to commit?"

"By promising to retail one-third of my wears."

"Oh. Well, you gotta do, what you gotta do." I sat on the bed, and Pam plopped down beside me.

"So, how was Philly?" she asked.

"We got an extension on the account."

"That's great. Daddy sent the right person."

I nodded and wondered if that were true. If only Winthrop knew the circumstances he had sent me to deal with, maybe all these new issues would have never risen, I thought.

"Anyway, after tonight, I'ma give Mario my sweet ass to kiss. Promoter hell." Pam rose just as I was about to spill my guts. My words were still stuck in my throat when she stripped naked, pushed me onto my back and straddled me. "Speaking of sweet asses to kiss. You missed me?" she asked.

"Mm-hm," I lied.

"How much?" she teased, kissing me across my face and down my neck.

I laid there, staring at the ceiling, searching for an opportunity to tell her that I needed space. Her lips were soft. Cold. Her pecks had begun to serve a purpose as they wandered across my chest then lingered at my belly.

"I've been waiting for you," she mumbled. Her fingers tugged at my sweats while her kisses relayed messages to my nerves, caused my body to submit to her will. Everything I had wanted to say became lost in her touching me. I groaned when her fingers found me, and my eyes shut. I tangled my fingers in the silkiness of her hair then cringed at the tiny kisses she was smothering my member with. Her lips had warmed around me, and in the quietness, I listened to her slurps and suckles. I gasped and pushed her head off of me. I wanted her to stop so that I could say what I needed to.

Pam was determined. Her licking her way back up my torso caused me to allow her to continue. Then, she raised her hips over me and lowered herself. "Aaaahhh," she gasped. Her eyes rolled into her head and I felt her quiver as she proceeded to milk me. Only her hips rotated in smooth, practiced rhythms and her fingernails dug deep into my pecks.

I gripped her waist out of habit and found myself diving deeper into ecstasy.

She leaned forward and kissed me, sucked my tongue like it was taffy and quickened her rhythm. Then she slowed and groaned, her rotations suddenly became an easy ride, and she threw her head back to gasp, hummed until her hips remained still. Again, she leaned forward and whispered, "I want it in my ass."

I tried to catch my breath. "What?" I managed.

"You heard me."

Indeed, I had heard her.

Still straddling me, she reached into the drawer of the bedside table and pulled out a tube of KY Jelly.

"What's that for?" I stammered; my eyes glued to the tube.

"Don't tell me you haven't thought about getting some peanut butter before?" she mused.

I was speechless, unable to figure out if Pam were serious or not. When she opened the tube, I knew that she was. "Come on, girl. That's not even my twist."

She lifted off of me and laid on her belly. She was smiling ear to ear. "I know we haven't talked about it, but I'm curious."

"Curious?"

"Yeah. It's something I've been wanting to try." I sat up and stared down at her.

"Why all of a sudden you're curious?"

"It's no big deal, Wesley. Everybody's doing it."

I stood and headed for the bathroom. "Not me."

Disappointment covered Pam's face. "What's the big deal? It's not like you'll be feeling the pain."

I closed the bathroom door behind me. It wasn't that I was unwilling to experiment. It was more because I've been trying to find an opportunity to break up with Pam. Trying anything that might create more of a commitment to her was out of the question.

I was under the shower when Pam entered the bathroom. She climbed into the shower with me. Innocence covered her face, but her smile was more of a smirk. "You are so old fashioned," she said pointedly.

"I'm not old fashion. I'm just not into that."

She began soaping my semi-hard member. "You should be flattered that I wanna give my entire body to you."

I turned my back to her and breathed deeply while she nestled against me. "What about giving me your heart, Pam? It's like all we have is sex carrying us."

"Uh-uh. I know you didn't go there."

I stepped out of the shower and noticed that Pam was staring.

"What's your problem, Wesley?"

"I don't have a problem."

She followed me into the bedroom. "Talk to me, Wesley. Is something on your mind?"

I knew that the opportunity I've been waiting for had come, the chance to tell her how and why my life feels so unfulfilled, how I wanted some space out of our relationship. I toweled off and pulled on my sweats.

Pam stood dripping water onto the carpet. "Well?" she asked.

"Well, what?"

"What do you mean all we have is sex?"

"Because it is."

"The hell it is! All I asked is to try something new, something different for a change other than the same boring shit."

Pam's tone struck a chord in me more so than her words. "Oh, so now sex with me is boring, huh?"

"That's not what I meant."

"That's what you said."

"Well, it's not what I mean."

I grabbed my Nikes and sox. "You wanna know what bothers me, Pam? I work my ass off to love you and all you seem to care about is sex."

She stormed across the room to the closet. "Ha! If that were true, then we would've been through!"

"And what do you mean by that?"

"I mean if it wasn't for me loving you, you'd probably still be in Philly with your brother, selling drugs."

"Selling drugs?"

She wrapped a bath towel around herself. "Yes, selling drugs. Who the hell you think trusted you enough to put you in the position that you're in? Me. That's who!"

"So now you've been carrying me?"

She spun and flagged me. "You know what, Wesley…I don't even know where you're going with this, but I'm not even gonna trip." She entered the closet.

I followed her, stopped short of entering. She had her back to me. "Pam, I'm moving back to Philly."

She stopped fumbling with her clothes and faced me. "Back to Philly?"

I nodded. "Yeah. I've been thinking about it for a while."

"Is that what this is all about? You wanna move back to Philly?"

I stood quietly, ready to absorb Pam's fury.

"Just like that, huh. And what about me? Your job? Daddy? You just gonna up and leave?"

"I can't do this anymore, Pam. Something's missing from my life."

"Well, get a dog!" she shouted. "You don't…uh-uh. You can't be serious about this."

"I am." I turned and crossed the bedroom with Pam on my heels.

"You probably got some bitch in Philly, don't you? All of a sudden you go to some fucking wedding and now it's over, huh?"

I grabbed my keys from the foyer table.

She blocked the door with her hands covering her face.

She began sobbing. "I'm sorry, Wesley. I didn't mean it. Whatever you want I'll do. Just don't walk out of this door."

I stood there, trying to piece together the puzzle that had me so confused. I grabbed for the doorknob, but Pam grabbed me.

"Please, baby, don't. I can change. I swear I can." Tears were falling from her eyes in puddles, and she was clinging to me for dear life… "I swear I'll change, baby. I swear."

CHAPTER 19

CAROL

I had wanted to take an extended vacation from work, however, I had just gotten my new job and felt well enough to return to work after only a week of rest and healing. Although the pain medication prescribed keeps me a bit drowsy, I've been able to function, acceptably, and deal with the issues which needed the most attention.

Occasionally, life wings a sucker punch at you, a test. That's how I've rationalized my situation, as another episode in a lifelong struggle and I wasn't about to throw the towel in on my dreams. My short vacation had given me time to reflect on life, period. Tonya's cussing me out each morning and evening had something to do with my decision too. I'd conclude that: I might have to limit myself in extending a helping hand to my students, something that, for me, will be certainly complicated. My children's welfare will have to become my priority and taking unnecessary risks out of that realm will only jeopardize their futures.

"Are you listening?" Kyle asked from across the desk.

I refocused my attention back to the teen. "Of course, I am," I responded while adjusting my arm in its sling.

Kyle Dixon, an eighth grader, has a problem keeping his hands out of students' bookbags. Mr. Epps had sent him to speak with me a half hour ago and Kyle hasn't stopped talking since. "I need you to do me a favor, Kyle," I said.

"Like what?"

"Put yourself in someone else's position. How would you feel if somebody stole something from you?"

"That ain't gonna happen."

"And why is that?"

"'Cause I ain't got nuttin' for 'em to steal."

"Alright. How about if they stole something from your mother?"

He shrugged. "Ain't nuttin' I can do 'bout that."

"But how would you feel?"

"I probably be mad."

"Okay then. Don't you think others feel the same way?"

"I guess. I don't know."

"Let me put it this way: are you trying to do prison time?"

"No. "

"Then that's exactly where you're headed if you continue taking from people."

Kyle shifted in his seat. "Prison don't scare me."

"Not now maybe, but it's still where you're headed if you don't knock it off." I sensed Kyle was picturing himself behind bars. His stare was distant. "Kyle, we won't continue tolerating you stealing from the other students. Mr. Epps has been considerate enough to have already given you two chances, but I'm almost certain you won't be given another. Fortunately, you're on your way to being kicked out of this school. You do know that don't you?"

He gave me a somber nod.

"Well, I hope so. And with you being warned, there's really nothing more that I can say. You'll have to do the rest. Understood?"

Again, he nodded.

"Good. I 'm through for now."

I walked with Kyle to the door. When I opened it, Felicia was standing there with a weak smile. Our eyes met then hers dropped to the floor. I tried to remain nonchalant and excuse Kyle; nevertheless, I walked from the door, leaving it open for Felicia who shuffled inside. She closed the door behind herself while I parked myself behind the desk and waited for her to speak.

"Are you okay?" she asked taking the seat across the desk.

"I'm fine. What can I do for you?" I asked impatiently.

"I just wanted to…uhm…see if you, uh, needed any help doing something. I know your arm is in that thing."

"Help doing something?"

"Yeah. And to say that I'm, uhm…really sorry about everything that's happened."

"You mean me getting shot? Or you giving me your behind to kiss?"

"It wasn't like that."

"Then what was it like, Felicia?"

Her eyes drifted from me. I wondered if she were concerned for me or more with herself. Either way, my frustration with Felicia has amounted to where involvement, outside of a professional relationship, has become an association that I would rather not deal with.

"I messed up," she simply said. "I'm sorry I didn't trust you."

"I'm sorry, too, Felicia."

We were silent a moment then Felicia stood and stomped for the door.

"Felicia, wait!"

She spun towards me and I pointed to the chair. "Have a seat. Please?"

Reluctantly, she did as I asked.

I exhaled in frustration. "Felicia, just because I'm disappointed in your decisions right now, doesn't mean that I'll always be or that I don't care what you do with your life. But you also have to care."

"I do care."

"Then you have to make decisions like you care. Chasing behind Hasim isn't one."

"You don't have to worry about me and Hasim anymore."

"No?"

"He locked up."

"For the shooting?"

"Drugs and the shootout. The baby will be grown by the time he get out."

"I'm sorry for you, Felicia."

"You don't have to be. I knew he was gonna get locked up one day."

"So, where you staying at now?"

"With my girlfriend, Peaches."

"And school?"

She sucked her teeth. "Don't worry. I'ma finish school."

"You sure?"

She nodded. "I'm sure."

"That's smart of you. Well, you know if things start to get hectic then there are programs that will help?"

"I know. You already gave me those brochures."

I wondered if she had read the brochures or was, she just saying what she believes I want to hear. I turned the conversation to finances.

"What are you going to do for money, Felicia? Hasim won't be there and boosting's certainly out of the question."

"I'ma have'ta get a job somewhere."

"Honey, you're only thirteen. There aren't many jobs out there for a girl your age." I came from behind the desk and stood beside her. "I'll tell you what I'll do for you. I'll look into several options that are available to you, but just know that DHS will need to be involved in order to provide most of the support — at least until you're eighteen."

"I'm not tryna go to no girls home."

"You won't have to, Felicia."

Skepticism covered her face. "They always be tryna put people in shelters."

"Not if you have a guardian, someone who's willing to look after you."

"But that's just it. I don't."

"Not yet. But if you do this for yourself then it's possible that some woman may be willing to forgive you for getting her nearly killed." I smiled and Felicia's eyes became starlight bright. She leaped from her chair and hugged me.

"Ow, owl My arm, girl," I gasped then gently hugged her, too.

Once again, my emotions had gotten the best of me. I didn't completely understand and in some way, couldn't believe that I'd volunteered to take on the responsibility for Felicia, but I had -- again. My past seems to always influence my decisions; plus, knowing the help she'll need to trek the tough road ahead of her was, basically, all that it had taken to influence my decision. Even so, I felt satisfied with my choice. My primary reasoning for taking this job in the first place was and still is to help needy children succeed in life, to take a vested interest in their well-being, something I had needed as a child. I genuinely believe that Felicia has the potential -- with guidance of course -- to make a difference once she overcomes her own obstacles. Nowadays, in a generation that has bred so many young mothers, plenty grown folks need to step forward and accept some of the burden of responsibility for lacks in parenting. I only recall what and who I needed while growing up. I've never been one to find the strength to turn my back on a child in obvious need of my help.

It was after 3pm when I locked my office door and was headed home. Mrs. Burns was in her classroom erasing the chalkboard when she noticed me standing in her doorway.

"Can I speak with you a moment," I asked her.

"Chile, bring your behind in here." She clapped two erasers together over a wastebasket then fanned through the cloud of chalk residue floating in the air. She placed the erasers on the chalkboard's ledge then wiped her hands with a napkin before taking a seat at her desk.

I sat in one of the student desks.

"I wish you would've come to me before you started chasing behind that child," she said, pointing to my injury.

"It probably wouldn't've mattered."

She sighed. "Probably not. You young ones have your own ways of motivating yourselves. So much energy. But I'm sure that's not what you wanted to talk about."

"Well, kind of."

"Who are needs rescuing now?"

I bit my bottom lip. "Felicia came to see me this morning."

"Sad and apologetic probably. They always are, you know."

"Mrs. Burns, this child has a good heart."

"I'm sure she does. So, why are you here?"

"Because I've decided to act as guardian for her; well, sort of, and want to know if I'll run in trouble with the Board."

"Guardian? What are you trying to do? Get counselor of the year already?"

"No. But…"

She raised a finger to interrupt. "Let me say this, Carol: You can preach to these children til' you blue in the face and just when you think they're listening, some rap star will come out with a song, some new cultural ideology will spring up and snatch their attention away from you. They're young and impressionable and if you believe that your problems won't get worst, they will."

"But don't you believe that not trying to help will hurt more?"

"Of course, I do. But, Carol, your purpose is to guide their adolescence is not their best friend." She breathed deeply. "Carol, I don't want to discourage you simply because you're only one step in the door, but I'd be doing you a huge disservice if I don't prepare you for more disappointment."

"I believe I'm a good judge of character, especially children. I do have three of my own, you know."

"Honey, they are all of our children."

Mrs. Burns' last statement nearly surprised me. I've always been under the impression that she wanted no real ties with any of the students. "But do you think the school board will have a problem with me helping this girl?"

"Not as long as you notify Child Welfare, and they agree that you'll be a great prospect. But who cares about how the Board feels? If you are strongly committed to helping her, then do it. You're not breaking any ethical clauses that you can't get around. You're caring. That's what we educators do."

I sat there confused by Mrs. Burns' compassion. I had thought that she would hit the ceiling after finding out what I intended to do on Felicia's behalf. I guessed that, for Mrs. Burns, it's a love/hate relationship with the students. On one hand she loves the promise they present. On the other hand, she despises the process of having sift through the bad to get to the good.

Mrs. Burns and I spoke for another fifteen minutes before heading outside to the parking lot where her battered Ford was parked. We departed with a light hug and she told me that she was thankful to have someone on staff who genuinely cares about the students. I headed towards the front of the school, smiling to myself and satisfied, had just come in view of my car when I saw them lingering beside the Nissan. Kevin and Wesley were there talking. They stopped when they saw me, and a thick cloak of seriousness hung amidst the early evening's air.

"What's this?" I asked when I reached them.

Kevin was first to speak. He was positioned between us like a referee instructing two prize fighters. "Mom, don't be mad."

My eyes darted from Kevin to Wesley back to Kevin. "Why would I be mad?" I turned back to Wesley in wonderment.

"Wes told me everything."

"Everything?" I questioned skeptically.

Wesley nodded.

"Yeah. Everything. He told me how me being in this chair was an accident, about how he's changed, about how he feels about you and everything. I forgave him, Mom."

"Kevin, I'm sorry," I mumbled.

"Sorry for what?"

Wesley touched Kevin's shoulder as if it were his turn to speak. "Carol, I've been wanting to come clean for years. I hope you aren't upset over me telling him."

The embarrassment of having held the secret from Kevin for so many years was stifling, yet a relief. I kneeled beside Kevin and held his hand. "Baby, I'm so sorry that I never told you."

"I know, Mom."

"I only wanted to protect you."

"But now you don't have to. I'm not a baby anymore. I just want you to be happy."

"You're right. You're not a child anymore." I stood and looked at Wesley, not sure how to deal with his initiative to reveal the truth to Kevin.

Kevin nudged me toward Wesley who was standing there with uncertainty pasted on his face. I said the first thing that came to mind.

"Are you staying?" I asked.

He smiled while nodding. "I'm not going anywhere."

"What about Atlanta?"

He reached into his jacket pocket and pulled out a tiny case. He snapped it open to display a huge diamond ring. "There is no Atlanta."

I looked to Kevin's huge smile, back to the ring, then into Wesley's eyes. My dreams seem to sparkle in them, and I wasn't about to allow those dreams to slip away again. "Can you take us home?" I asked, fighting back my tears of joy.

"Without an answer?"

"Isn't it obvious, Wesley? Yes. Yes. Yes."

In all my years of seeking true happiness, I would have never guessed I'd have to work so hard and wait so long for it to arrive. Taking a chance on someone has always come to me like second nature. I think it's about time I take a chance on me, to find my true happiness.

THE END

www.ingramcontent.com/pod-product-compliance
Lightning Source LLC
Chambersburg PA
CBHW021156110726
47900CB00002B/603